Knight to Remember

Maxine Douglas

Also by Maxine Douglas

Widows of Blessings Valley Series

Elizabeth

Vera

Men of the Double K Series

Red River Crossing

Winds of Change

Game of Chance (2025)

Brides Along the Chisholm Trail Series

The Reluctant Bride

The Marshal's Bride

The Cattleman's Bride

Nashville Duets Series

Nashville Rising Star

Nashville by Morning

American Historical / Gilded Age Romance

Leanna's Light (Book 12, Alphabet Mail-Order Brides)

Victoria (Book 19, Angel Creek Christmas Brides)

Hannah's Discovery (Reclusive Man Series)

Kit's Brides (Double Trouble series, December 2024)

Blood Ties

Contemporary Romance

The Gingerbread Inn (Christmas at the Inn Series)

Rings of Paradise

Knight to Remember

YA Cozy Mystery

Reading, Writing and Catmetic (Holiday Pet Sleuth Mysteries)

DEDICATION

For my grand-daughters:
Courtney Ann,
may you find your knight in shining armor one day and always believe
in your dreams.
Makenna Marie,
who has more strength in her body and soul than any knight could
possibly hope for.
I love you both.

ACKNOWLEDGMENT

Thank you to the re-enactors of the Bristol Renfaire in Wisconsin. Your authenticity was a great help in my journey to write this book.

CHAPTER ONE

England, 15th Century

"Black Knight, pledge thy loyalty and love to me and no other!" Queen Isabel Trenowyth demanded.

"I cannot, Your Grace," the Black Knight replied, ignoring her haughty tone while holding back his jet-black Andalusian from prancing too close to the queen and her court. "My heart belongs to another."

"Another? Thou wearest the colors of this kingdom. *My* kingdom." Isabel snorted, her proud face suffused with rage. "Thy heart canst belong to no other in this time or in any other time."

"Thou speakest the truth. I wear the black and gold colors of Heartsease as a knight by my own pledge, sworn to protect the castle walls and its people, nothing more, Your Grace. I cannot give my heart to one who on a whim hast so many knights on bended knee." The Black Knight backed his snorting stallion a little farther from the anger of Queen Isabel. He'd vowed to protect Heartsease and its lands for longer than the queen's reign; he'd never promised to be her lover.

"Of course, there are other willing knights of Heartsease who would give me the pleasure I request. It is what thou hast refused me all these years which I seek. I have offered thee everything, and now thee shall have nothing." Isabel waved him off like a finished piece of meat. "The tournament shall continue."

A sneer marred her otherwise beautiful face. "Ruin him, Sir Thomas!" Queen Isabel commanded of the Black Knight's opponent.

Sir Thomas backed his gray mount away from Queen Isabel until he reined in solidly beside the Black Knight. The line had been drawn, and the Black Knight knew Isabel would not take lightly a refusal from two of her knights.

"My Queen, I cannot. I have given my life to protect the people of thy kingdom. Heartsease is the place of my birth and that of my family before me. Our alliance to thy father before his death is long and unquestionable. It will continue as such. On this day, I refuse to take the Black Knight's life to ease thy pride and bruised heart," Sir Thomas replied, loudly enough for half of Heartsease to hear him.

"Thomas, thy protection of me is admirable but not needed," the Black Knight rebutted under his arnet to his childhood friend and then turned to the queen. Her furor over Thomas's refusal was evident and so would be her vengeance. He couldn't allow Thomas to face her wrath. "I refuse Sir Thomas's protection and challenge him to *Joust a' Plaisance.*"

Queen Isabel thought for a moment before coolly signaling for the Chief Marshall to approach her. A wicked smile crossed her lips as she whispered into his ear. A look of dismay soon turned to pleasure as the Chief Marshall faced the Black Knight and Sir Thomas.

"These are the queen's terms of the challenge set forth. If the Black Knight loses, he will remove the coat of arms signifying his alliance with Heartsease and be banished from these lands for all time. If he should be the victor, then Sir Thomas will be stripped of knighthood and work the land as his father before him. In addition, the Black Knight shall do the queen's bidding day and night as Queen Isabel so chooses."

A hush fell over the list as all in attendance waited for the Black Knight's answer to the cruel request. If he accepted this challenge and lost, he'd be forced to leave his homeland forever. This was the place of his birth and the birth of his beloved Catherine. His victory would bring shame upon Thomas and his family and devastate them, and he'd be at Isabel's mercy for the rest of his days. Either way, he was doomed. The queen left him without a true choice.

The Black Knight backed his black steed, turned, and then trotted around the list toward William, his young squire. Passing along the rail, he paused long enough to take up the lace-and-purple-ribboned offering from Catherine, the beautiful daughter of Heartsease's dressmaker. He leaned in toward the raven-haired, blue-eyed young woman, his heart already hers. She smiled and tied the token around his lance, making him her champion.

"How can I help but not fail, Catherine," he whispered to the lovely but plainly dressed maiden.

"I know not, but thou wilt find a way to right this wrong," she said, a trusting smile brightening her worried face. Touched by her faith in him, he rode off to the east end of the list, doom flittering down his spine. The only honorable way out would be to lose, even though it went against his nature, and he could possibly lose Catherine as well.

"Sir Reynold?" William queried.

He gave his squire a confidant smile, seeing the fear in the boy's eyes. "I will not allow the queen to dictate my life any longer, my young friend. If I must leave my home and country to save Thomas's family name, I will." Reynold dismounted and handed the reins to William.

"The queen would rather see thee dead, sir," William commented, leading the stallion alongside Reynold toward their tent.

"Beware what thou sayest, young William. In this court, even the ground hast ears," Reynold cautioned his bold squire, placing a hand on the young man's shoulder. "Lest thou take care in those words, or it could be thee riding Abraxas and carrying a lance against thy father instead of me."

"What of my cousin?" William tethered Abraxas to a post outside their tent. "What will become of Catherine if thou art no longer here to protect her?"

"Catherine knows I'd not bring shame on thy family name. I will find a home and send for her when the time is right." Reynold walked into his tent to prepare for his joust against Thomas, his blood brother and childhood friend. "Wherefore Isabel hast chosen this course now is beyond my knowledge, Will. Her jealousy runs deeper since her father's death."

"Some say that Isabel hast consulted the stones. They say the stones have foreseen thy failure and disappearance from Heartsease, Reynold," Will said in a hushed tone, as if afraid to be heard by anyone but himself. "Father is fearful that Isabel plays with the darkness of life to rid thee of thine. Her witch is powerful in the black arts."

Reynold handed his arnet to Will, shook his head, and took a deep breath. It confirmed his own thoughts. "I have heard the same words whispered behind tankards of ale. It is more than my life she yearns to rid me of, it is my will to refuse her advances and physical pleasures."

REYNOLD PULLED HIMSELF into the saddle and waited for Will to hand him his shield and cronel-tipped lance. Much was at stake in this event. At the other end of the list, his oldest and closest friend waited for their time at the joust.

They all had grown up together—Thomas Astley, Catherine, Isabel, and he. Thomas was the son of a farmer, and his cousin, Catherine, was the dressmaker's middle daughter who was more of a tomboy than a girl. As a child, Isabel hadn't known the difference in their positions in life. Her father, King David, had allowed her to play with the children of Heartsease. She'd been a big-hearted girl, filled with passion and love. Reynold had been the king's eyes and ears even as a boy, up until the king's death when Isabel was but an enthusiastic girl of sixteen. Something inside her changed that day—something dark and evil.

At one time in Reynold's life, he had thought he loved Isabel. These past years with her ruling cruelly as queen made him realize that Catherine, and not the selfish woman Isabel had become, had his heart.

After years of fulfilling the promise he'd made to Isabel's father as he lay dying, Reynold continuously refused the provocative suggestions Isabel presented him on a regular basis. He'd promised the king he'd defend Heartsease and look after Isabel, not become a bed toy for her to play with like so many others. Isabel proved to need no looking after; she had plenty of willing knights to defend her honor and visit her private quarters.

The sound of trumpets brought him back to the present and the task awaiting him. His plan was a simple one that he'd have to conceal from Will. If he didn't, the young squire would find a way to inform his father of Reynold's planned deception.

Reynold spurred Abraxas ahead and entered the list at the east end at the same time Thomas did from the west end. They'd been through this many times before on the practice field. Abraxas stomped in eagerness to charge, and Reynold spurred the stallion forward.

Galloping toward Thomas on the opposite side of the tilt, Reynold felt the jolt of the lance against his chest. He'd hit Thomas but not enough to knock him off his mount.

Gathering himself, he repositioned the lance and charged toward Thomas again. As they met in the middle of the tilt, Reynold lowered his weapon at the last moment and felt the jolt of Thomas's lance hit him squarely in the chest, causing him to teeter in the saddle. The cheers of the crowd echoed inside his arnet, vibrating in his ears.

One more pass, and it would be over.

Ignoring Will's questioning look, Reynold spurred Abraxas around and charged his lifelong friend for what he prayed would be the last time. When the two passed, Thomas lifted his lance, missing Reynold by inches. Knowing in that instant Thomas was no fool, Reynold fell sideways, allowing Abraxas to drag him to the west end of the list.

The pain shooting through his body was nothing compared to the satisfaction of knowing Thomas would continue his life as a knight. His plan may not have worked to perfection, but his honor to Thomas was held intact. Reynold would find a new life—a lonely one but a life nonetheless.

"Whoa! Whoa!"

The words came through the blackness trying to take claim to his mind. Abraxas suddenly halted, and Reynold felt himself lifted off the ground. Someone took his foot from the stirrup and pulled the arnet from his head.

Focusing, he gazed into the eyes of his raven-haired love. He had indeed found his place, at last, in Catherine's arms.

CHAPTER TWO

United States, 21st Century

Courtney Parker took her place in the stands near Queen Victoria's court. Her role as dressmaker to the Queen of Heartsease afforded her one of the best seats on the grounds, and she never missed a joust.

The opening ceremonies for the Bristol Renfaire season were being held today, and there was a large crowd of onlookers. It was a time everyone looked forward to and yet dreaded. Early Monday morning, they'd all have to return to the twenty-first century, leaving behind a period in time each reenactor loved so dearly.

One of the first jousts of the summer was about to take place between the mysterious Black Knight and one of the regular jousters. Each year, they brought in someone new to play the part of the banished knight of Heartsease. It was a mythical story she never grew tired of and loved dearly.

To her dismay, this year would have a different ending. The Black Knight would be banished this year for good, making way for a new program next season. Courtney was saddened to see the love story end.

Legend had it that the Black Knight had refused Queen Isabel's advances once too often, having professed his love for another. Queen Isabel Trenowyth, in her fury, gave an order for his destruction during a joust that would either send him from his beloved Heartsease forever or strip his childhood friend of his knighthood. It was told that the Black Knight disappeared, leaving behind his love and family, never to be seen again. In all the historical books she'd read and the tales she'd heard, not once was the knight's given name ever mentioned. He was simply known as The Black Knight of Heartsease.

There was one book portraying the life in Heartsease that had escaped her. The mysterious single volume was a hard find, and one she'd hoped Samuel, the bookseller of the fair, would be able to locate for her. It was said to be printed in the handwriting of its author. The book thus far was just a rumor—a rumor the existence of which her heart held hope in verifying. This season could be her last chance at getting it.

The fate of the actor playing the Black Knight would end in a flourish. He would ride out of the village, never to be seen again. Courtney's heart ached when she thought of not living the touching story again the following season. She still hadn't decided whether she would have the heart to return to Bristol the following year.

The two knights now in the arena were on their last pass, when the Black Knight lost his balance and slid off the side of his horse, hanging from a stirrup. His foot lodged in the foothold, he tried to keep from hitting the ground while his horse galloped across the field in a panic.

There was something wrong; he seemed lifeless to Courtney. A collective gasp drew the onlookers into an eerie silence. Courtney left her seat and ran to the stable entrance.

If the man is hurt, she may be able to...to what?

She wasn't a first aid staffer, yet there had to be some way she could lend a helping hand.

Thinking quickly, one of the other knights stepped in front of the black charging horse, waving his arms and yelling "whoa." The Andalusian slowed enough for someone to reach up and grab the reins, bringing the horse to a jolting halt.

Courtney ran to the hanging knight's side, helping to lower him onto the ground. She unbuckled the armor, removing it from on top of his still body, pulling the black arnet off. A mass of long, dark hair fell freely into the dirt. She pushed the wet strands from his face and held her breath as she gazed at his fluttering eyelids. Thick, blunt, dark lashes were like raven wings on his pale cheeks. When they opened, she peered into eyes the color of whiskey, drinking in their depths.

The cloud of darkness attempting to take the man faded slightly in his eyes as he stirred. His color brightened, turning to a deep tan as life came back into him. Her heartbeat accelerated with a strange sense of recognition as their souls met and then returned abruptly to its normal beat. Whatever she thought she saw disappeared in the blink of an eye.

"CATHERINE." THE NAME but a whisper—Reynold strained to focus more clearly on the blurred pretty face looming over him. Her touch was the same, soft and soothing, her scent that of lavender and all woman.

"He's not bleeding; that much is good. There doesn't appear to be anything broken."

The voice, a sweet melody of verse to his ears, seemed a little deeper than he remembered and muddled. The words sounded strange. Was she so upset by his falling off his horse that she'd become hysterical? He tried to move, groaning as his head ached as if he'd been hit with a club. Something lightly touched the back of his head, tender and small in its exploration, and he realized it was her delicate hand.

"I don't feel a bump, but that doesn't mean..."

Reynold blinked again to focus on the blurry face. "Catherine?" He brought her image into focus with a jolt to his memory of her. The woman leaning over him was disheveled, her dark hair escaping from her headpiece, framing her brown eyes and pink cheeks. He could see the fear in her eyes. He wanted to tell her to fear not, but his tongue was thick in his mouth.

"Don't talk. We've got to have the paramedics look you over before you can move."

"Para..."

What is this woman saying? It sounds like the Queen's English but not entirely so.

Reynold pushed away the two masked men dressed in white grabbing his arms.

Part of Queen Isabel's army of men, if one may call them men.

"Thou goatish elf-skinned pigeon-egged priest. Keep thy hands off me." Reynold rolled, getting to one knee, and then rose to both feet. The world around him spun slowly when he sensed the woman taking hold of his arm. He could smell her scent. Without even looking at her, he knew who she was.

He looked down into a pair of chocolate eyes he could swim in forever, only to find they were void of the love he'd seen in them just minutes before the joust started.

How could I have thought this be my Catherine when I find nothing familiar in her eyes?

"You better sit down for a while. Let me take you to my shop in the village where you can sit and rest."

"Nay, I must attend to Abraxas." Reynold looked around the list's west entrance for Abraxas. A horse like his didn't go with just any man. No, Abraxas belonged to him heart and soul. They'd saved each other's hide on more than one occasion. "My armor. Where is my armor?"

"We've taken him to the stables where he'll be cooled down, fed, and watered. He seemed a little unnerved by your fall." A young squire bearing the colors of Heartsease stood before him. It wasn't the face of young Will, but there was something familiar in his eyes. "Your armor will be there, as well as your tack."

"What is't they call thee?" Reynold allowed himself to be led up the hill in the direction of the village.

"Will, sir, I am the son of Sir Thomas and thy squire." The young man looked at him with confusion in his eyes. "Dost thou not remember, Sir Black Knight?"

Reynold looked at the knights and ladies standing around him as they waited for his answer. They were watching him cautiously, and he knew he had to tread carefully. How could he remember this young squire as Will when he not only looked nothing like him but would have addressed him with his given name?

He pushed through his comrades, finally noticing the strange-looking people gathered around the list fencing—women and men dressed in scanty attire, their limbs bared.

Something is amiss here, yet everything looks the same.

The list remained the same. Queen Isabel and her court sat where they always did, but he couldn't get a good look at her in the shadows. Was she sitting there gloating over the spell she'd cast that changed Catherine and his squire?

What bit of black magic has Isabel wrought this time? Which one of her witches has she used to replace Catherine's love in hopes of making me her own? I must use caution or fall to her desires.

He ran his hand along the base of his neck. Relief flooded him to find his amulet still intact. "Aye, Will, I remember. Attend to Abraxas in the stables after putting my weapons away." Reynold gave the squire a pat and sent him on his way. God help the boy if Abraxas sensed anything amiss.

"Aye, Black Knight," Will said, picking up the broken lance from on the ground.

"Do not forget the extra apple for Abraxas...he hast earned it this day," Reynold called after him, following close behind the woman he'd initially thought to be Catherine.

"Whoever taught you to ride?" the woman asked, leading Reynold up the hill toward her shop in the main village. "From what I saw, you have no business being on a horse, much less jousting."

What kind of insult is this?

"I'll have thee know, I am the best horseman in the land," Reynold stated, pushing her arm off his shoulder. "And I need no woman to help me move about."

"Maybe not, but you sure couldn't prove it by me. You're weaving about like a drunkard with little sense of direction."

"I need to find the dressmaker to the queen," he said, turning up the dirt path toward the heart of the village. "I thought it may be thee, but now, I think not."

Her breath hitched inward, and her step slowed with caution. "Why? Surely she can be of no help to you." Suspicion edged her voice. She knew more than she wanted him to believe; her eyes revealed she held secrets unknown to even herself.

Reynold halted, spinning the woman around so he could see her face. He wanted his meaning to be clear with no question of his intention. "Ah, she is all that I need now or ever."

The shock in her eyes was mixed with yearning, as if she wished it to be true. He didn't know the woman. Such fancy on her part was unwarranted and certainly unwanted.

Reynold glanced past her shoulder, confused by the look of recognition in her eyes. As luck would have it, they'd stopped in front of a shop bearing a sign reading QUEEN'S DRESSMAKER.

The dresses hanging just inside the doorway had a special touch to them. Even from this distance, Reynold recognized the work to be that of Catherine's. No other dressmaker in all of Heartsease had her exquisite stitching ability.

"Catherine!" he half-whispered. Forgetting about the maddening woman, he stepped up on the stoop of the shop.

"There's no one here by that name, Sir Knight." A young shop girl sauntered up to Reynold, her bosom spilling over the bodice of her dress. "If a Catherine's who thou seekest, I can be that desire thou hath."

He frowned at the wench's bawdy tone. He had no time to play with her. "Is this not the shop of the queen's dressmaker? It is she I seek."

How could this not be Catherine's shop when the stitching clearly states otherwise? Another trick of Isabel's to make me believe I have gone mad. Her magic must have grown powerful over the years. I'll not underestimate her again once I am returned to my homeland.

"Yes, sir. This is the shop of the queen's dressmaker, but no lady by the name of Catherine works here. The queen's dressmaker stands just behind you." The lass pointed to someone behind him. At long last he'd hold Catherine in his arms, never to let her go again.

THE BLACK KNIGHT TURNED swiftly, the light and softness in his eyes immediately replaced by the dark coldness of suspicion. In only two long strides, he reached Courtney, fire burning in his molten eyes.

"Thou wilt tell me what thou hast done with my Catherine," he demanded, shaking her almost senseless.

Courtney winced at the pain of his grip on her arms. She took a ragged breath to steel herself against the anger in his eyes. There was a storm brewing behind his incredible, sensual, amber eyes—a golden storm filled with warmth that sent a cold chill through her.

What in those eyes scares me—the depth of their sensuality, or the fact that I could drown in them without a care? Or is it that I feel I know him deep down in my soul?

"Lady Courtney, do you need assistance to your shop?"

Sir Thomas! Thank goodness.

A wave of relief filled her body as she breathed in to steel her quaking nerves. Saved from drowning for the moment, she pulled free of the Black Knight's grasp.

"Sir Thomas, I believe the Black Knight may have hit his head harder than first believed. He insists a lady named Catherine is dressmaker to Queen Victoria," Courtney said, moving into his shielding presence. No one would dare go against Thomas; his sense of protection over her was well known throughout the reenactors. Over the years, they had become close friends but nothing more.

"Sir, I can assure you Lady Courtney is the mistress of this shop and dressmaker to Queen Victoria." Sir Thomas's words seemed to be all that was needed to still the mysterious man dressed in the colors of

Heartsease.

"Sir Thomas Astley of Kent, on the lands of Heartsease?"

"Yes, sir. Have we met before? Perhaps over a glass of ale at the Black Swan?"

"Thomas, dost thou not recognize me? It is I, Reynold. Thy son, William, is my squire." Reynold took one step forward. Courtney saw the warning flash quickly in Thomas's eyes and prayed the mysterious knight did, also. For his own good, if nothing else.

Courtney relaxed slightly when Reynold stopped inches short of Thomas. She wasn't sure why, but the thought of these two fighting sent a shiver of dread through her.

"Forgive me, sir. Perhaps m'lady is correct, and I did receive a blow to the head. I beg thy leave, Lady Courtney."

Reynold bowed and backed up, keeping an eye on Sir Thomas. Turning, he walked past the dress shop, giving it one final look.

"What was that all about?" Thomas whispered into Courtney's ear as he escorted her into her shop.

Her gaze never left the retreating backside of Reynold as he headed down the path toward the stables. From the stoop of her shop, she could see the wet strands of his black hair slide across his back from shoulder to shoulder. She wondered what his hair would feel like against her skin, all wet and silky. The thought sent a hot shiver shooting through her body, leaving her craving a complete stranger.

"I thought you knew." Courtney stepped upon the wooden floor, losing sight of the mysterious knight called Reynold.

"No, they never told me they'd replaced Joe with this new guy." Thomas whispered so the paying customers didn't hearing him speak in modern English. "I asked around in the stables about Joe, and no one's heard from him."

"Something's not right, Thomas. This man who calls himself Reynold is either an excellent character actor, or he lives this way of life to its fullest."

Courtney walked to the back of her dress shop and through the door leading to her sewing room. Even though this *faire* only operated during the weekends for eight weeks out of the summer months, she could always count on doing her sewing during the weekdays. She needed the sense of calmness pushing a needle and thread into fabric gave her.

"Agreed. This man seems to have an infatuation with you and your shop. Only it's with someone named Catherine. Take heed of him, Courtney," Thomas warned as he left her to her sewing.

"Noted, Thomas. I know where to find you if need be, have no fear," she reassured him, running the needle and thread through the fabric in her hand. Sewing by hand and creating costumes from another time always relaxed her while she mulled things over.

It had been the lure of the story of Heartsease that brought her to southern Wisconsin a few years before. When she'd heard they were going to reenact the legend she felt a kinship with, she immediately contacted the organizer to secure a shop in the village. Soon, she found a small place out in the country nearby where she could continue to practice her dressmaking craft during the off-season.

Pushing the needle halfway through, she couldn't chase away the feeling of having met Reynold somewhere before.

Maybe at another Renfaire years ago?

Could it have been in Minnesota where she performed her craft for many years, before settling in comfort here near Bristol?

No, she would have remembered those golden eyes and long black hair, not to mention the way he looked at her as if he knew everything about her. And that horse of his... Not many reenactors could afford an Andalusian, let alone one as magnificent as his.

This Black Knight was hiding from something, and Courtney meant to find out exactly what.

CHAPTER THREE

"Which of Isabel's sorceresses has she consulted to place this spell over me?" Reynold mumbled, walking absentmindedly on the village road. "She hates me that much for thwarting her sexual advances? How could she—oomph!"

Reynold looked squarely into the eyes of the man who looked like his childhood friend. They stood toe-to-toe, neither giving away anything to the other. It was Thomas on the outside, but nothing in his eyes revealed the man Reynold had come to love throughout life.

"Just who are you, and what have you done with the man who was supposed to be in the arena and not you?" Thomas stood his mark and blocked Reynold's way when he tried to go around him. "What the hell happened to Joe? And who in the hell hired you to replace him?"

"Thomas, I have no quarrel with thee. I know not this Joe or what hast become of him. I am but a man on a journey not of my own making." Reynold walked to a log bench under a nearby tree and took a seat. The shade would cool the heat burning his body but do nothing for the fire burning in his heart.

Do I speak the truth? Mayhap? Nay! 'Tis the work of Isabel's black magic which has placed me in this enchanted village. Did my deception backfire, sending everyone dear to me into a different world where I am a knight unknown to those around me?

Lifting the corner of chain mail, Reynold pulled the protective covering over his head. The additional weight of the metal did nothing to help his light-headedness. No, it was the cause of a journey he did not ask for. The Heartsease he'd grown up in as a boy lay before him, yet it did not.

"You will address me as 'Sir Thomas' when we are out among the people." Thomas loomed over him, his hand ready on his sword. "Now, answer my question, or I shall run you through."

"How can I give thee the answer thou seekest when I know not what it may be? Please, sit down." Reynold motioned toward the other end of the log bench as an invitation for Thomas to join him. How would he broach the subject of who he was? He didn't even know where he was, let alone how he got here.

Thomas declined the invitation, making no move to come closer to Reynold. "Just tell me what happened to Joe. That's all I ask."

"M'friend, let me tell thee a story. In it, thou may find thy answer." Reynold sighed, and gathering his belongings, he stood once more. "Come, walk with me."

Reynold took only a few steps before Thomas walked beside him. "This day we...err, I, was on my horse in the midst of a joust with my childhood friend. I had rejected the advances of my queen one too many times and pledged my love to another...her dressmaker, Catherine..."

When there was no response from Thomas, Reynold wondered whether he were the crazed one. Maybe it had been his memory that Isabel altered and not that of his blood brother and the people dearest to his heart.

Could it be Catherine never existed, and Lady Courtney is anything but the love of my soul? Nay! I will have no other. Catherine and Lady Courtney must be the same maiden.

His heart pounded warmth to his loins at the very thought. His heart was true and would not be deceived, that he was sure of. There would be only one way to find out...

A kiss never lies.

They walked in silence for several minutes until they heard the neigh and snort of Abraxas, along with the screams of scattering men from the stable. The black Andalusian charged out the stable door and into the list.

Reynold gave a trilling whistle, stopping the steed in his tracks.

"Abraxas can sense things are not as they once were." Reynold jogged down the hill, jumped the fence, and waited for his trusted friend to come to his side.

"WE ARE IN A STRANGE land, my friend." Reynold stroked his snorting stallion's neck, soothing his nervousness with the gentle touch. With a handful of mane, he guided the horse back to the stables where his squire stood just inside the barn door, arms crossed and shaking his head.

"You said one apple. That damn horse wanted the whole barrel." Will stepped aside as Reynold and Abraxas came through the opening.

Reynold laughed hardily, slapping the animal on the rump as it went into an open stall. "He dost have a need to taste their sweetness. I'm afraid I have spoiled him endlessly with them."

"In all my years of doing these faires, I've never seen a horse like him." Will walked alongside Reynold as he went over to check his tack. "Where did you have him trained?"

"I trained him myself, Will. You accompanied me on many trips to the training ring." Reynold wiped the dust from his saddle and then draped the bridle over the cantle.

Will stood next to him, looking at him as if he were crazy. "Sorry, I've never seen that horse or you before today." Will stepped away from Reynold. "I think you banged your head pretty good and should go to the emergency room."

"Emergency room? What is an emergency room?" Reynold asked.

"You've got to be kidding me." Will backed closer to the barn door opening. "Oh, I get it. You can turn off the dialog now. We're all reenactors here; no civilians are present."

"Young Will, I do not understand the meaning of thy words." Reynold stood confused, wondering what manner of speech his squire spoke to him.

What has happened to my world? To my home and the life I once lived? Everything is so strange yet the same. Yet not.

"Let me try to explain it to him, George." Sir Thomas stood in the rays of the setting sun, his figure but a dark outline in the light.

"Sir Thomas, thou seekest me out. Could this mean thou dost remember, after all?" Reynold took several steps to Thomas, hoping things in his world were coming back to the way they should be.

"Ahhh...Sir Reynold." Thomas stepped completely through the door and stood next to Abraxas's stall door. "I was hoping you would join me at the Black Swan for a glass of ale."

Finally.

"My friend, I would gladly join thee." Reynold placed a hand on Thomas's shoulder, grabbing his forearm with the other.

COURTNEY WATCHED FROM the stoop of her dress shop as Reynold stopped the monstrous horse in his tracks. She'd never seen anything like it before, and she'd been around a number of well-trained horses through the years.

As mysterious as the man was, there did seem to be something vaguely familiar about him. She just couldn't put her finger on it. Though she felt positive she'd never met him before, something in her heart had sprung when he'd opened those golden eyes of his.

She'd felt herself sink into their warm depths with an ease she'd never known before—familiar warmth, which touched her soul, if only for a brief moment. It was probably her romantic notions about the story of Heartsease that sparked her feelings, not the man himself. For pity sake, she didn't even know what that knight in the story looked like under his armor. She'd never found a picture of him anywhere.

Courtney turned away from the man and his horse, returning to the business of her dress shop and the few customers still milling about.

There was so much left to do before the end of the season. She still had several orders to fill from the end of last season to get underway, as well as deciding just how she was going to pack up everything for the move to her modern home.

She didn't look forward to a long, cold winter without the friendship and laughter the faire provided during the summer. She often marveled at how paying customers came dressed in costumes resembling anything from Vikings to Robin Hood to harem girls. This was a place where a person left the modern world behind in exchange for a simpler way of life. It was a place of fairy tales come true, and every little girl was a princess in search of her knight in shining armor.

Maybe her knight had finally found his way out of her dreams and into her world.

CHAPTER FOUR

Reynold followed Thomas down the path in the direction of the Black Swan not knowing whether he was friend or foe. If he was back in his homeland, there'd be no question. Here in a land that looked like Heartsease but wasn't, Reynold couldn't be sure of anyone other than himself…including the woman who may possibly hold his heart in the palm of her hand.

Lady Courtney stirred him deep in his soul. Nothing about her said she could be Catherine, yet every ounce of his heart told him she was his love. His groin had responded in lust to only one woman, until he'd looked into the sweet brown eyes of Lady Courtney.

Even the people of Heartsease were different to him—especially in their manner of speech and dress. There were women dressed with their bodies barely covered, while others wore short pants and sandals. Their speech seemed close enough to his own that he'd been able to pick up words here and there when he'd been close enough to hear them. The now-thinning crowd moved toward the top of the hill, and shop lanterns were going out as evening fell upon the village.

Looking to the graying sky, Reynold felt dark forces beyond his control had landed him in a strange land. For now, he'd return to the stables to find a comfortable place to bed down for the night.

Once daylight breaks, I'll search out the village sorceress and reverse Isabel's spell, no matter the cost.

"Reynold!"

The sound of his name floated through the air like the soft wings of an angel. Reynold turned to find Lady Courtney a few yards from him. Her skirts gathered in her hands and the hem brushing the tops of her ankles, she was as beautiful as the stars on a clear spring night…all fresh and new, holding the promise of a warm summer season.

"Lady Courtney." Reynold nodded, stepping up alongside her. A scent as familiar to him as breathing wafted past his nose, bringing forth an image of Catherine. Lavender assaulted his memory and fired his longing for a woman now lost to him. Lady Courtney, who insisted she wasn't his beloved, was more like Catherine than she knew. More than Reynold wanted her to be.

The color of her hair and eyes may have changed, but the passion for life sparkled just below the surface. If she came any nearer, he'd cover her face with gentle kisses until the pulse in her neck encouraged him to continue on.

"Do...you..." Her chest heaved as she tried to catch her breath and talk at the same time. Reynold stood mesmerized by her flushed cheeks. Skirts still gathered in her hands, she finished. "Have...a place to stay?"

Reynold felt Sir Thomas at his back. As much as he'd prefer a bed with a soft woman in it, he knew in his heart Lady Courtney wasn't that type of woman. And in this strange land, he wasn't sure there'd be a woman he'd want to bed down with for the night, anyway. He'd never taken up with a wench before. He was not about to start. If his heart wasn't in it, neither was his cock.

"Lady Courtney, I must protest!" Sir Thomas stood off to the side, yet close enough to intervene.

Chuckling, Reynold shook his head. "Once again, thou come between us with no cause, my friend. I shall sleep with Abraxas this night, m'lady." He bowed slightly, his gaze never leaving her sparkling brown eyes. Full of need for her, he wanted to reach out and take her fully with his lips, to claim her as his own before Sir Thomas could draw his sword from its sheath.

Lady Courtney stood so close; he could almost feel her skin upon his. "If you'd rather sleep with the horses on a bale of hay, that's totally up to you. I just wanted to extend the offer, nothing more."

"M'lady, thy offer is welcome, but not one I shall take up on this night." He turned back toward the path leading down to the tavern. He may not have needed the ale before, but he certainly did now. Only the lovely Lady Courtney could put out the fire burning deep in his loins, but the promise of a cool tankard would have to suffice.

"Sir Thomas, thou mentioned a tankard of ale?" he called out, not daring to look back, fearful he just may reconsider the lady's offer of a bed.

SIR THOMAS GRABBED Courtney's arm, making her cringe in pain. "What the hell are you thinking, Courtney? You don't know this guy from Adam, and you were just about to invite him into your home as if he were an old friend. At least the man had good sense to decline before you lost more than the offer leaving your lips."

"Let go of me, Thomas! It's none of your business who I do or do not invite to my home." She pulled away from him, rubbing the life back into her arm. "It's not as if I'm inviting him into my bed!"

"He's a man, for God's sake. What would you expect him to think of an offer such as that from a beautiful woman?" Thomas stepped closer to her, his breath fluttering across her face. "I'm only trying to protect you, Courtney. For all we know, he killed Joe and buried him out in the old corn field."

She'd never seen Thomas act like a jealous boyfriend before, and he had no call to start now. "If you're so worried about it, then maybe you should get a beer and find out why he's here? Besides, the man can't sleep in the barn. Can you imagine how stiff he'll be in the morning? Not to mention smelling like hay and horses."

"If he stayed with you in your shop, he'd be stiff, all right, and not from sleeping on a few bales of hay." Thomas laughed, pulling Courtney into his arms.

"You are such an ass!" She smacked him in the chest and then turned on her heel. His continued laughter followed her up the path to her dress shop. "Men! Scoundrels, the lot of them."

Thomas is right. How could I even consider offering my home to a man I've never seen before? He could be an escaped convict in disguise, for all I know.

She turned to watch the two men meander down the path.

Great. Now he's got me picturing a mass murderer instead of a lost soul.

As they strolled side-by-side, they reminded her of two old friends out for a night on the town. Warmth spread over her heart, melting the fear Thomas had tried to instill in her. Reynold was lost. She felt it deep in her soul.

"So, that's the mysterious Black Knight I hear everyone's been jabbering about."

Isabel Cummings!

Courtney stopped dead in her tracks. Holding a conversation of any kind with the faire's newest resident and self-proclaimed witch was not something she wanted at the moment...or any other moment, as far as that went. The woman sent a chill of dread up her spine whenever she came out of her shop. Courtney could almost see the black cloud of doom hovering over her.

"So it seems," she answered, taking a step forward in hopes of escaping the red-haired potions shopkeeper. Issie, as she liked to be called, had a reputation for bedding men and either spitting them out or turning them into her little pets. She'd sent more than one good man whimpering off into the night, tongue dragging on the ground like a fool.

"Does he remind you of anyone, Courtney? Isn't he the most delicious male specimen you've ever seen?" An outrageously beautiful woman, Issie licked her lips like a cat after drinking a bowl of milk... Or one about to chase down a newly discovered mouse.

"Don't you have enough puppets in your collection, Issie? Or could it be you're tiring of the same old blood night after night? After all, there's not much of a challenge around these parts, is there? At least none with a thread of common sense when it comes to you. I don't think he's your type."

Shit! She's done it again. Why do I let this woman get under my skin? It's like she's got some magical power.

Courtney hated the way Issie got to her without even a second thought. It was as if she knew exactly how to get her riled up. Every anger button she had, Issie knew exactly when and how to push. Until Issie's interest in him, she hadn't even known she had a sensitive button where the Black Knight was concerned.

"I heard you ran to his side, Courtney. Is that true?" The words dripped with venomous poison, and Issie's black eyes seemed to burn with the fire of jealousy. Maybe it was the uncommon combination of red hair and black eyes that gave her the look of a woman possessed.

"The man was hanging from his stirrup, Issie. What would you have me do, leave him there to possibly get trampled on?" Courtney shook her head then turned away from the woman. She wanted to escape Isabel Cummings before the shadows of the night settled in too close. A cold chill sent her skin crawling over her bones.

"He's a good rider, and Abraxas wouldn't have stepped on him. They are almost one and the same, those two." Issie's voice, a mere whisper through the breeze, swirled through the air into Courtney's ear.

"What?" Courtney turned on her heel and marched up to Issie's stoop. The woman obviously thought she possessed inside information, and Courtney wanted it. "And just how would you know that, Isabel Cummings? He's a stranger to everyone here."

"Ha! There are many things I know, Ms. Courtney Parker. The night has many eyes and ears, and I listen closely to the whispers of the night." Issie's gaze continued to follow Thomas and Reynold through the shadows forming as the sun set in the West. "Take care, Lady Courtney, for on this night, a true knight has arrived in this make-believe world of Heartsease. Your safe little world is about to take a tumble."

Issie's laugh was what Courtney could only describe as a witch's cackle, full of evil. It sent goose bumps racing up her spine, raising the hairs on the back of her neck.

THOMAS'S LAUGHTER FOLLOWED Reynold down the hill. He was sure that whatever Thomas found so funny, the Lady Courtney did not. At least, that's the way it would have been between Thomas and Catherine. They may have only been cousins, but they acted more like a big brother teasing his little sister. If his observation were true, it was the same between Thomas and Lady Courtney. Somehow, it brought comfort to him knowing that Thomas looked after the fair maiden.

Mayhap not all has been lost.

Hearing Thomas's footsteps crackle on the ground, Reynold slowed his pace.

Before this night passed, I will convince Thomas my words are true. That I have nothing to gain by telling lies about our relationship.

Any why would he lie? He loved Thomas like a brother and had given his own life to save that of Thomas. Or at least he'd thought he had. Instead, a spell of black magic had been cast over them. He would survive this the way he'd survived many other things in his life—with strength, patience, and cunning to recognize the way to a victorious outcome...even when all seems lost.

"Curse Queen Isabel and her..."

"Be careful what you say, Reynold." Thomas walked along beside him, the warning clear in his eyes. "This may be a place of make-believe where actors come to play, but even the night has ears. Don't be so easily fooled by what you see and hear. There are many here who wouldn't hesitate to shove a knife in your back if it furthered their position. Figuratively speaking that is."

Reynold paused at the tavern door. "Surely you jest. I can defend myself fairly well, Thomas. Hast thou forgotten I am an expert at the knife, and no man has been able to best me, although many have tried? These men seem soft to me, compared to the knights I've dealt with."

"I have no doubt that you are an expert and believe you are far more superior than the men here." Thomas chuckled. "However, I'm not so sure if you're capable of defending yourself against the simple act of deception."

'Tis true. Isabel's deception hast undone me.

Conceding to his friend, Reynold let out a long, heavy sigh. "Thou art correct. I am a trusting soul."

Reynold followed Thomas through the tavern door. It may have looked the same, but there, the similarity ended. The atmosphere didn't carry the same odor of flickering flames from the lanterns. The smell of smoke and perfume mingled with spilled ale, while the conversations of the men and women stopped on a dime the second he closed the door. He wasn't used to the whispering and curious looks directed his way. No, he was more accustomed to being welcomed wherever he went, not looked upon with suspicion as he was here.

"Thomas?" Reynold pulled out a chair so his back would be to the wall, concerned that when he sat, the men staring would attack him. "Do I need to take heed whilst drinking?"

"No." Thomas laughed, sitting in the chair opposite Reynold. "They're just as curious as I am about you. And you can cut the period language; the fair has closed for the night."

Period language?

Reynold shook his head. "I speak the queen's language, Thomas. Thou dost well to speak nothing but."

Thomas pushed himself up away from the table, chuckling. "You are a piece of work. Now, what kind of beer do you like?"

What kind? There is now more than one to choose from?

"Is there not one type?"

"You're right. A light ale it is!" Thomas walked over to the innkeeper.

This is strange, indeed. Different ales. Different manners in which a peasant may speak. What spell hast this country fallen under? Isabel's witch must be more powerful than I thought.

Reynold looked at the strangely shaped bottle Thomas placed in front of him. It looked more like a flagon used by a sorceress, filled with a golden liquid potion, than something he should drink of his own free will. He watched Thomas lift the bottle to his lips and take a long swallow, pleasure filtering around his face.

"Ahhh." Thomas licked his lips, placing the bottle back on the table. "Nothing like a cold one at the end of a hot summer day."

Reynold wrapped his fingers around the chilled bottle, slowing lifting it to his lips. He took a swig and promptly spewed the bittersweet light golden liquid from his mouth.

A drink that looks like pee yet has the light taste of honey. Nothing like the sweeter, heavier ales of home.

Reynold tipped the bottle back again, this time letting the brew swirl in his mouth before swallowing it. Satisfied with the feeling of the liquid slipping down his throat, Reynold took several more long gulps of the brew.

"Hold on there, buddy, you'll get drunker than a skunk drinking that hard and fast." Thomas laughed, shaking his head. "Ever hear of the word, 'moderation'?"

Reynold wiped his hand across his mouth, placing the empty bottle on the table. "Nay, this tastes more like honeyed water than ale."

"So, are you going to tell me just who in the hell you are? Or am I going to have to get you drunk to loosen up your lips?" Thomas leaned into the table, his gaze boring a hole into Reynold. All traces of friendliness disappeared. Questions, speculation, and warning darkened his face now. It was a look Reynold had grown to respect and take heed of through their friendship.

"What thou wilt hear will not only surprise thee but also cause thee to believe I am a man filled with lies. As a knight of Heartsease, 'tis not in my soul to tell a tale of lies." Reynold sighed, knowing he'd have to tread lightly. "My name is Sir Reynold Loddington, and I am best known through the land as the Black Knight. As a young boy, the King of Heartsease, David Trenowyth, befriended me after my family died of ergotism. We are like brothers, Thomas. I am betrothed to your cousin, Catherine. We all grew up playing in the castle and on its grounds as if we belonged there. King David longed for his only daughter, a willful child, to have passion for the people she'd one day rule over. As thou knowest, she possesseth passion but not in the manner in which her father had hoped."

Reynold sat back in his chair as Thomas stood. Rolling the empty beer bottle in his hands, uncertain of how much more to tell him, Reynold wished he'd never accepted the joust as presented. If he could go back and change things, he would. That choice didn't seem to present itself to him then, nor did it now. He'd not known what his act of deception in the joust would cost him or those close to him.

"This calls for a heavier drink, and one that is more fitting to this incredible conversation." Thomas went to the bar, leaving Reynold wondering whether he'd done the right thing. What if he'd told more than was needed? Or hadn't said enough to convince Thomas he spoke the truth and wasn't a crazed man on the loose. He didn't blame Thomas for not believing him; he wasn't sure he'd be any different if the situation were reversed.

A woman's shadowed figure caught the corner of Reynold's eye the moment she stepped through the door. Her fiery-red hair seemed to glow like a beacon in the night. She scanned the room before locking her cave-like eyes onto his. The magnitude of their depths pulled his gaze deeper into hers with a snapping force. Darkness enveloping him, his heart and stomach lurched all at once.

The thud of a tanker and the splash of ale hitting the table brought him from the murky depths. "Just so I understand. You say we were childhood friends in England during the fifteenth century?"

Reynold nodded his head, drawing in a deep breath and feeling a small sense of relief. "Aye, m'friend. We have known each other a long time." Reynold glanced back to the door and found the woman gone. He settled back into the chair, feeling quite certain the night played a trick on his mind.

More black magic since arriving in this strange place.

"Thomas, aren't you going to introduce me?"

Reynold peeked up from his tankard of ale. His gaze caught a delicate hand on Thomas's shoulder, a blood-red ring carrying the insignia of Heartsease on the right ring finger.

Queen Isabel!

CHAPTER FIVE

Reynold jumped to his feet and bowed to the woman he'd called "Queen" these past three years. "Your Majesty."

Thomas's hearty laugh filled the tavern. "Reynold, this one is anything but royalty here. Stop embarrassing yourself and sit down. Everyone's watching you."

Ignoring Thomas's insult, the woman extended her right hand to Reynold.

"Since Thomas has such a foul tongue and appears to have lost his manners, allow me to introduce myself. I'm Isabel Cummings, but you can call me Issie, if you wish." Amusement flickered in her otherwise black eyes, as if she found the situation a piece of entertainment for her and her court.

Cummings? Issie? She took on the surname of her chambermaid?

Reynold had taken her hand in his and bent to kiss her ring when Thomas elbowed her in the side, knocking her off balance.

"Thomas!" Reynold hissed, amazed his friend would treat their queen in such a manner.

"Your presence is not welcomed here, Issie. Find another fool who'll bend to your wishes. There's not one here." Nose wrinkled in disdain, Thomas pushed away from the table, leaving Reynold to deal with Isabel on his own. As during their entire life, he was the only one who could soothe her rage.

"Thou must forgive my friend. As thou knowest, Thomas forgets his place from time to time." Reynold waited in silence for Isabel to take a seat at the table. "Reynold Loddington, at Your Majesty's service."

Thomas's disrespect for their queen troubled his mind but not as much as the manner in which Isabel was dressed. The woman who lavished upon herself the finest fabrics and jewels now resembled a peasant, rather than a woman who ruled cruelly over her country and its people. With so much that had changed, could it be Isabel, herself, had changed, as well? Could she actually have found the compassion for her people that her father had?

Possible, but not bloody likely.

There was a time when Queen Isabel would have had one of her own people flogged for speaking to her in such a way. The Isabel who now sat in the chair once occupied by Thomas had turned a cheek and dismissed the slight with a wave of her hand. Something was terribly amiss, and the thought of what it could be soured Reynold's soul to the core.

"Oh, that? I'm used to it. He's just a little boy who wants the candy in the jar but can't have any," Issie retorted, motioning for Reynold to sit, as well. "So, tell me about yourself, Reynold Loddington."

"Yes, please do tell us." Courtney stood next to the table, Thomas flanking her right. Her eyes lit up the room with warmth and compassion.

Reynold shifted in his seat to ease the growth between his legs.

"Look who I found lurking in the shadows." Thomas smiled at Issie like the Cheshire cat.

The two women eyed each other, contempt in Issie's eyes and distrust in Courtney's. Deep beneath the surface of politeness lay a rivalry with which Reynold was already all too familiar. These two had never liked each other, even as children playing in the courtyard.

He couldn't accept the fact Lady Courtney was not his Catherine. Something deep down in his heart and soul told him they were one and the same, just born in different worlds and time.

Reynold stood, allowing Lady Courtney to take his seat. He'd already told Thomas his story. What more could he say? That he was in love with a woman much like Lady Courtney? That he'd been banished from his homeland because he wouldn't bed down with his queen?

Not with Queen Isabel sitting in front of him; he valued his life too much for such an accusation...even if it were the truth and common knowledge within Heartsease. She wouldn't hesitate to have him cut down where he stood, if she so desired.

And what of Lady Courtney? Would she believe his words, or treat him with the kindness she'd shown the mindless of their country? He'd not take the chance; not yet any way.

"Reynold Loddington." His name rolled like sweet honey off Courtney's lips. "Very unusual. Is it an old family name?"

Reynold shifted his feet, not sure how to answer Lady Courtney's question. If she were really Catherine in another time, then wouldn't she have full knowledge of who he was? Her face was the same porcelain hue, and while her eyes may have changed in color, he saw the same passion and sweetness within them. He wondered whether her lips still held their sweet taste, as well.

Issie cleared her throat, drawing everyone's attention back to her. "I would venture to guess his parents were deep into fifteenth century England history. I'd also bet that—"

"Enough, Issie! I don't think this man needs to be subjected to your questions, ladies. It's late, and we all need to be fresh for tomorrow's crowd." Thomas slapped Reynold on the back, and then led him toward the door and into the safety of the night.

"FARE THEE WELL, BLACK Knight!" Issie called out, waving her hand in the air as Reynold and Thomas took their leave.

"Well! I never." Courtney sat back in her chair, amazed at the turn of events. Here sat Issie Cummings, self-proclaimed witch, with one man lapping up her every word while another spat at her. Just what the hell did she have that no other woman had, anyway? That she didn't have?

"Of course you have." Issie continued waving, her eyes never leaving the backsides of the two men until they were through the door. "More times than I'd care to recall."

"Issie, you are the most...ohhhhh! I can't even begin to describe how nasty you can be." Courtney looked at her, watching her expression change from lustful to predatory. The cold, black look sent a chill of recognition down her spine. She's seen the look before, but she wasn't sure when or where.

Issie took a drink from Reynold's tankard, licking her lips slowly. She reminded Courtney of a lioness finishing her evening snack. Only the purr of satisfaction was missing. As far as Courtney was concerned, the woman had no business taking such a liberty. She was being far too familiar with Reynold Loddington for Courtney's liking.

Then again, why should she give a darn? He was just another reenactor, here for the summer, and gone as soon as possible after Labor Day weekend. No, she didn't care what happened to Reynold Loddington. At least, that's what she kept telling her heart each time his name floated off of Issie's lips.

Issie leaned forward, her eyes burning like black flames. "You and I have never liked each other, Courtney." She slapped her hand down on the table hard enough to upset one of the tankards, spilling ale onto the table. "I will have what I set out to get, and you'll not stop me this time around, Catherine!"

A shiver of fear and warning flittered down Courtney's spine.

That's the second time today someone's called me Catherine. These people have got to get their minds straight.

"I don't know who Catherine is, but she's not me. I wish you and that Mr. Reynold Loddington, or whatever it is he's calling himself, would get that straight." Courtney shoved herself out of her chair to leave the table. She leaned down, coming nose-to-nose with her enemy. "You'll not scare me, Isabel Cummings. I know your kind, and there's a reason why other women avoid you."

Courtney stomped out the tavern door, Issie's wicked laughter following her into the night.

THERE MUST BE A FULL moon tonight, and I just missed it.

Courtney looked to the night sky but found only a sliver of moon hanging there, shrouded by wispy clouds.

Nope, no crazy people out according to that moon. I think the night holds a pack full of lies about that myth because crazy has hit here in full force...full moon or not.

Cackling laughter swirled around her like a mini whirlwind. Dark foreboding streaked through her soul. The high-pitched noise held a sinister edge to it, much like that of the Wicked Witch of the West in the movie version of *The Wizard of Oz.*

As quickly as she'd felt trapped, the sensation left her standing in the warmth of the summer night once again.

"Damnable woman!" Courtney hiked her skirts as she marched up the darkened path to her shop. "Who in the hell is this Reynold Loddington anyway?" She sputtered to herself, her gaze never leaving her moving feet. "There's an answer to this somewhere. I just have to find it before it drives me insane."

She searched her mind, trying to break through the cloud of confusion edged with the suspicion instilled by Issie. Why had the woman singled her out now? They'd always been distantly cordial to one another, yet never really spoken or taken the time to get to know one another. Tonight, they'd said more to each other than they had the past few months while setting up for the current season.

Being a new vendor to the fair this year, Issie Cummings had made more enemies in thirty days than a person could in a lifetime. Her air of superiority may have attracted single-minded men, but it did nothing to form a sisterhood with any of the women. Courtney was amazed at how Issie could so easily go from sultry vixen to bitch in accordance with who walked into her shop or crossed her path in the streets of

Heartsease.

Now it seemed she'd set her vixen sights on the faire's mysterious knight. She already had him melting on her every word and movement. Geez! From the way Reynold acted, it was as if he thought she was the faire's queen instead of Victoria.

Bowing and calling her "Your Majesty" the way Reynold did had caught both Thomas and her off guard. And heaven knew Issie didn't need any encouragement. By the look of what had taken place in the tavern, Reynold's treatment of Issie only gave her more of an uppity air than she already possessed.

Reaching the stoop to her shop, Courtney glanced at the lights blazing in Issie's potion shop. Somehow the slippery woman had gotten past her on the path. She was about as mysterious as Reynold.

Things can only get better from this point, can't they?

After all, the season was underway, and there'd be enough to keep her busy and not thinking about Issie Cummings or Reynold Loddington. At least while he was not in her sight or hanging around Thomas.

Yet, there had to be a connection between the knight and the witch. That hint of recognition she'd seen flit across his dark-gold eyes could only mean one thing. Reynold thought he knew Issie from somewhere. Courtney thought it had to be from another renaissance faire. Maybe in another place, she played the queen of that fair, and he'd just been showing respect to her in that capacity.

As if hearing her thoughts, a willowy shadow passed by the window shades. A chill crept up Courtney's spine. Somehow, she knew the answers to many of her questions could be found in that shop.

CHAPTER SIX

Reynold woke with Abraxas munching on the bale of hay he'd used as a bed last night. Pushing the horse's nose from his ear, Reynold rolled over. The pounding in his head quickly reminded him of the bittersweet ale he and Thomas had drunk after leaving the tavern. He'd only experienced the pain before if he'd been clonked on the head, not from drinking a few tankards of ale. What was in the drink that would cause him to feel as if his head were swimming in the castle moat?

The sound of hardy laughter coaxed his eyes to open further. "Can't sleep the day away, Reynold. The gates open at ten o'clock, and there's much to do. You need to get your ass off that bale of hay." Thomas kicked the stacked bales with the toe of his boot, jostling Reynold into the stall boards.

Swinging his legs off the bales, Reynold reached for his pants. "Thomas, thou couldst hear a cock crow before the sound came from the animal." Grimacing because of the heavy feeling between his eyes, Reynold pulled his pants up over his legs and then tugged on the boots designed to protect his legs from injury during battle.

"Good thing, too, or else you'd be without your breakfast." Thomas handed him a bag with a big red jester on it. "It's not much, but it'll do for now. I hope you like bagel-and-egg sandwiches. I thought this would be a good time to talk a bit while we got the horses ready."

Nodding, Reynold took the offering, pulled the bag apart, and ripped the paper off the covered sandwich. Turning the bagel over, he brought the sandwich to his nose and sniffed before biting into the barely warm food. The food just another indication of how far he was from his homeland. What he wouldn't give for a bowl of salmagundi and a slice of bannock.

Thomas stroked Abraxas's neck, and the horse nuzzled his head against his chest. "Why isn't he like this with everyone? I heard he caused a ruckus in here last night, aging your squire by ten years."

Swallowing hard, Reynold wiped the corner of his mouth. "He knows thee, Thomas. Abraxas remembers thy smell from when he was foaled. You saved his life pulling him from the womb of his dam."

Thomas shook his head. "You've got to be kidding, Reynold. I'm lucky I can groom, saddle, and ride a horse, let alone assist in a birth."

Reynold shoved the last of his sandwich into his mouth and then cupped his hands into a bucket of water. After several swigs, he wiped his hands across his thighs, hoping his next meal would be a bit more succulent. "Thou didst, and I am forever grateful. I would have lost both the foal and the mare if thou had not come into the stable when thou didst.

"He needs to run, Thomas. Is there a field nearby?" Reynold opened the stall door, allowing Abraxas out. "By the look on thy face, I would say not. The list, then."

With Abraxas at his shoulder, Reynold walked past Thomas and out the barn door. A soft pat on the neck, and Abraxas burst through the open gate into the arena. The midnight-black stallion bucked and reared before cantering around the fence, releasing all the pent-up energy from being confined all night in a stall—something he was far from used to, having been raised in the open fields surrounding the castle of Heartsease.

Reynold and Thomas stood in silence, admiring the sleek animal before them. Reynold shrilled quickly, and Abraxas halted in midair and then moved in a slow trot over to them.

Reynold stroked his horse's nose, giving him the apple he'd hidden in the waist of his pants. "Thy surname is Astley, Thomas. Thy name comes from a descendant of a powerful English landowner whose eldest son, thee, became a knight in the court of David Trenowyth, King of Heartsease. A position in life thou desirest even now."

"How in the hell do you know that?" Thomas demanded, stepping away from the fence. "No one knows the truth that surrounds the myth, and no one knows my supposed family connection to that crazy myth. I'd like to keep it that way, if you don't mind, since it's nobody's business but my family's and mine. The last thing I need around here is for people to think I'm totally delusional."

The anger and fear in his voice did little to deter Reynold. He had to make Thomas understand he knew everything. Reynold needed his help in finding out why he'd been sent to this mirror image of the 1490s; for it had become clear, he was no longer in the place he'd been in at daybreak numerous mornings before.

"We grew up together, Thomas, and shared many secrets as young boys. I am betrothed to your cousin, Catherine. Or I was to be betrothed to her until Isabel's jealousy..."

Reynold retold his story from last night. If he was going to make Thomas remember, he'd have to tell him everything, not just a small portion, of the time between his family's first arrival in Heartsease to the time of the joust, which brought him here.

Thomas ran his hands over his face. "You really expect me to believe that bullshit? I thought you'd give that crap up after a few beers last night."

Reynold slapped Thomas on the back and then whistled to Abraxas. "Thou shalt believe, m'friend. Thy memory shall return. Then thou wilt know I speak the truth."

COURTNEY STOOD ON THE other side of the bleachers just behind Reynold and Thomas, but it was the jet-black animal that drew her attention. The magnificent Andalusian pranced around the arena, proudly displaying his flowing mane and tail. If a horse could be arrogant, this would be the one. He demanded attention without a person even realizing it.

As much as she'd tried to eavesdrop on the two men, the horse had captured and held her imagination. She could feel herself on its powerful back, sheltered in the arms of the Black Knight of Heartsease.

She rocked with the rhythm of the horse's canter, strong forearms wedging her between a pair of mail-covered arms. A black plume matching the blackness of the arnet flowed in the breeze—a perfect complement to that of the horse's tail. From under the metal headpiece, long hair fell over a broad width of shoulders. Courtney reached up and ran her fingers over the nicked metal. Slowly she lifted the front plate to see the eyes peeking through the narrow slats...

Trill!

Courtney blinked, catching her breath as she quickly inhaled. Her daydream vanished into the dreamy mist, along with it the identity of her black knight.

The Andalusian trotted to his master and nudged his shoulder with his nose. Reynold turned from Thomas and began walking along the fence with the horse by his side. When they reached the gate, Reynold opened it wide enough for his massive stallion to go unassisted from the arena into the stable.

Courtney closed her eyes, trying to recapture her vision from a moment ago. If only she could see his face... Even the books she'd collected over the years on the mythical land of Heartsease had no photo or rendition of his face based on legend.

If I could only recapture the vision for a few more moments...

"Impressive, isn't he?"

The voice faraway and vaguely familiar broke into her concentration.

Opening her eyes, Courtney floated on a cloud of desire. "Mmmm." It felt as if she were in one of her own dreams, watching her knight walking away on a pair of long, powerful legs.

What I wouldn't give to feel the strength of them wrapped around me, holding me tight against his body with intense power. To feel his lips on my...

"A man like him must have a betrothed, or at least a woman at every faire, wouldn't you think?"

The devouring feeling of desire vanished with the sound of Issie's voice. The sensual warmth that had touched her skittered away from the cold touch of the other woman's voice. "What have I done to deserve you hovering endlessly around me, Issie? Ever since Reynold Loddington showed up, I can't turn around without you lurking near me in one way or another."

"Like it or not, there's a strong connection between the two of you." Issie stood in front of Courtney, blocking from her sight what little remained of her view of the backside of Reynold. "And I, for one, don't like it. Never have and never will."

Courtney took a step backward, wanting to put a bit more distance between herself and the evil woman in front of her. She could feel deep in her soul that the woman held an aura of wickedness about her—black and murky.

Courtney's movement for protection of some sort from Issie did no good. Without physically moving, Issie drew closer to her until it felt as if she'd crawled right into her body, coaxing her to wilt under her icy touch. A cloak of malevolence filled her as something wicked tried to take a grip on her soul. Her heart thumped harder, fighting, flooding her blood with heat that chased the frosty touch of evil from her core.

Courtney drew upon her renewed strength, until a white light of protection surrounded her being. She didn't believe in magic or understand why the light was there, but it had chased Issie's darkness from her being. For that, she was thankful.

"Careful Issie, I hear the water in these parts can melt even the likes of you."

THOMAS WALKED UP THE incline, muttering under his breath.

"Something's got to be done about those two."

He'd been watching the two women, and their body language was anything but pleasant. Even a blind man could see the thin line of hatred barely separating them. He wasn't sure which one would draw first blood, but he had a feeling Issie wouldn't hesitate. She was that kind of woman, knew what she wanted, and went after it until it was hers...or destroyed it without guilt.

"Did someone ask for a drink of water?" Thomas lifted a full ladle from the bucket he'd grabbed hanging from a water spigot near one of the concession stands. "Might be the only time today you'll get one as fresh or as cold."

Issie whipped around, knocking the offering from his hand. "Some other time, Thomas," she hissed and then stomped away, her skirts swishing in the dewy grass.

"You really need to be careful, Issie. Water might be a precious commodity one day," he called out to the retreating figure as he brushed droplets of water from his tunic. "It should not be wasted so callously."

"Thomas, she's baiting you." Courtney's hand fell lightly on his arm.

"Yeah, I know." Thomas took her hand from his arm, squeezing it lightly. Smiling to ease the worry from her eyes, he knew there was an emotional storm on the horizon. Not knowing why or how, he couldn't help but feel he'd be drawn into the middle of it, whether he wanted to be or not.

Maybe the sudden change in the direction of the wind carried the warning stirring in his heart.

CHAPTER SEVEN

The trumpets' fanfare blared, announcing the gates to the faire would be opened soon. Reenactors hustled to get into their positions before the first visitors of the day arrived outside the gates. Shopkeepers opened their doors, and the faire's street merchants busied themselves on the grounds making last minute preparations, all getting ready for a step back into time.

Taking Courtney by the arm, Thomas led her up the incline to her shop. "What is it with you and Issie, Courtney?"

Courtney sighed deeply, and Thomas wished he could chase away the concern on her face. Her stormy relationship with Issie troubled him as much as it did her—most likely, more. Courtney was a woman everyone liked and called friend. Everyone, that was, except Issie Cummings.

"I wish I knew, Thomas. The woman has a way of getting under my skin, and I hate it. The more I try to resist, the deeper she gets to me."

Thomas shook his head and then slipped into the tongue of Heartsease. "Thy words are true, m'lady. But take heed. I fear thou hath found an enemy close to thee, and one which I fear will not disappear so easily."

Courtney nodded. "Thou speakest the truth, Sir Thomas. I shall heed thy warning and pray that no evil comes this day. Fare-thee-well."

"Fare-thee-well, Lady Courtney." Thomas nodded his approval and left Lady Courtney to ready her dress shop for the peasants about to enter their kingdom.

Smiling to himself, he still found it amazing how he could so easily slip from the language of one time period to another with the ease of breathing air. Many of the reenactors listened to speech CDs, studying the language day and night weeks before opening day ceremonies, while for Thomas, it came as a second language, as if he was born into it rather than centuries later in a different world, literally.

During these past few years at Bristol, it had been as if his family's incredibly insane stories about Heartsease were true. He felt like Peter Pan. This was Never Never Land, a place where all things were possible, and he never had to grow up. At least, not until the end of the season.

That's when the reality of the modern world set in. It was a world he wished could change back to medieval times, where life may have been harsher but was a lot simpler. That's why he'd become part of the Bristol family. It was his way of living in the world for a few months out of each summer.

"The time has come," was all his grandfather had to say when Thomas told him that first year he'd be spending most of the summer playing medieval make-believe. It was then Grandpa Will had dragged him up into the attic and pulled out the tattered journal he'd kept hidden in the floorboards. "Your destiny lies within these pages, boy." His eyes sparkling, Grandpa Will handed him the fragile leather journal. His fingers had tingled as he'd touched the worn leather, and a shiver had soared through him that touched his soul.

He'd all but forgotten about the book until Reynold showed up with his wild tale of Heartsease being an actual place in time. Even now, Reynold's words rang through his head.

"Thy memory shall return. Then thou wilt know I speak the truth."

"THOMAS! CANST THOU tell me what is the reason for the trumpeters?" Reynold shouted as he jogged up the path. "Is Heartsease under siege?"

"Attacked? Heavens, no, Sir Reynold. The gates are about to open so the peasants of this land may come inside." Thomas walked past Reynold without stopping.

Catching up to Thomas, his sword drawn and ready to defend his queen, Reynold looked back toward the gates. "The queen—she is not in danger?"

"Not hardly, Sir Reynold. Sheath thy weapon and come with me. There is much to do before the last joust of the day." Thomas started down the path toward the stable.

Following Thomas, Reynold tried to sort out the confusion flooding him. The more he struggled to understand this strange time, the more uncertainty gripped the edges of his mind.

I do not understand this world I am in. The trumpets blare with warning, and nothing seems amiss. The people walk about nearly unclothed. And no one knows who I am. Everything and everyone's amiss here.

Reynold slid his sword into its sheath but rested his hand on its pommel. If there was treachery within the walls of Heartsease, he'd be the first to cut it down. His oath to serve and protect carried on into this new land, even if Thomas insisted there was no need.

"Do you know the routine, Reynold?" Thomas asked, reaching the stable gates.

"I know not of what thou speakest, Thomas. What is ruuteen?" Reynold reached into a bucket of apples, grabbing one for Abraxas.

"Oh, boy." Thomas looked upward to the hayloft and then turned to face Reynold. "There will be three jousts today. The first will be a joust of skill, which goes to the Black Night; the second a joust of champions, I'll win; the third and final joust will put you and I against each other by order of Queen Victoria to break the tie of the first and second round of competition. This changes each day, giving each of the knights a turn at becoming Queen Victoria's champion. "

Reynold nodded his head, putting a brush to the back of his horse. "It shall all end one day soon; thee and I shall part without a word to one another."

"Not quite, Reynold. This act has taken place every weekend. It's a performance that we put on for the customers." Thomas grabbed his own grooming supplies and then stepped into his horse's stall. "In between jousts, we will walk the grounds, greet our fellow actors, and talk with the folks who have come to see us. You may even be asked to have your picture taken with someone, especially the ladies. They love the idea of a knight in shining armor at their side. A little something for them to show off to their friends in the office on Monday morning. They might even fantasize about what it would be like to have a knight of their own in their bed."

"Fantasize?" Reynold stopped brushing Abraxas, looking to Thomas for an explanation of yet another word he didn't understand.

Thomas laughed like a little boy. "They may dream about having...ah...a physical relationship with a knight. It's that whole little girl looking for her knight in shining armor. There aren't many out there, so they come here to make their night dreams more real."

"Thou speakest as if these maidens are wenches, Thomas. It would not surprise me if a lord or two came looking for thee." Reynold released the hoof he'd been picking. "If thou spoke of my daughter or sister in such a way, I would not hesitate to skin thee alive."

Thomas laughed. "You'll see what I mean before the end of the day, Reynold."

"I hope not." Grabbing his bridle, Reynold looked out the stable door. There were a few small groups of people sitting and watching as the queen's falconer displayed his birds of prey, explaining to them how each of the birds had a purpose. A woman screeched as a peregrine falcon flew into the stands, perching itself at the top of a pole just under the net covering, shielding out the sun's rays.

These people were indeed strange. Reynold didn't believe the audience held any real respect for the falconer or his birds. They were there only to tell a tale of what they'd seen today. He felt certain they didn't fully understand the impact these birds had on a falconer's survival...not to mention that of his hunting companions. Reynold turned away, his heart sitting heavy in his chest.

"I shall champion Queen Victoria?" Reynold slung the bridle over this shoulder and then began digging through the colors of material until he found his black-and-yellow caparison representing Heartsease. He may be one of Queen Isabel's knights, but he'd never champion her unless her life was in danger. Then, and only then, would it be his duty to do so.

Yet, that would never happen. The queen here was Queen Victoria, not Queen Isabel. He prayed Victoria treated her subjects with love and understanding, not with contempt as Isabel had.

Thomas swung his replica medieval war saddle onto his horse's back. "Being the Black Knight, you will always start out as her favorite...until the last joust of the day. That is when..."

"I deny her advances and take up the lace-and-purple-ribboned offering of the queen's dressmaker." Abraxas neighed with excitement. Reynold slid the bard over Abraxas's rump and then gently placed the wooden arcon war saddle upon his horse's back. As always, Abraxas danced with anticipation.

"Not long my friend, not long," he whispered into one of the horse's cocked ears.

"I thought you didn't know the routine, Reynold. You're jumping the gun, though." Thomas tightened the cinch on his saddle and then dropped a stirrup into place. "The offering from Lady Courtney will happen at the last joust of the season. Then the performance changes a little with—"

"Abraxas is ready today; he's been in this stall much too long." Reynold placed the curb bit in the horse's mouth and slid the headstall over his massive head. "Aye, I know what to do, Thomas. I have done the feat before, with a much different outcome, I can assure thee."

"Let's go then." Thomas led his gray gelding down the aisle, reins held loosely in his hand.

"Thomas, thee will need thy armor." Reynold began to buckle his breastplate into place.

"Not at this faire, Reynold. The first rounds of competition here is a carousel of horsemanship," Thomas called out over his shoulder.

"Horsemanship? Come Abraxas, thy must show them how a real joust is performed." Shaking his head, Reynold followed behind Thomas, fear gripping his heart. If things went as before, what time would he find himself in at the end of the day? Would he be returned to his beloved Catherine or left to endure more of Isabel's black magic in this strange world?

REYNOLD REACHED THE gates of the list to find it lacking a tilt. How could there be a proper joust without a tilt to separate them from either other? The lack of the tilt could cause opposing horses to run into each other.

Have these knights no love for their mounts?

He must find out more about this carousel Thomas spoke of; maybe there'd be an explanation in his words for the missing tilt.

"Thomas, what is this carousel of which thou speakest?" Reynold mounted Abraxas with one swift swoop. Even though the horse stood sixteen hands, Reynold's height matched it perfectly.

"The carousel is a match of skills. Generally, the lances aren't used to knock an opponent from this horse or to hurt anyone. There's no reason for a tilt until the end of the day at the final joust, when lances will come more into play." Thomas swung his leg over the cantle, sitting lightly in the saddle. "Think of it as a game, Reynold."

"A game for children, not knights." Reynold patted his anxious horse on the neck, feeling the horse's muscles tighten under him with anticipation mixing with that of his own. He was more than ready to get on with the day's events. Maybe if Issie—he still found it hard to address his former queen as Issie and not Isabel—was in attendance, she'd work her black magic and send him back where he belonged, instead of in this unfamiliar mirror image of his home.

"Just follow my lead, Reynold." Thomas spurred his horse into the list, leaving Reynold trying to figure out what was about to happen. He was a great horseman and had won many tournaments. Without a tilt, Abraxas could come to harm by a misaimed lance. He'd have to take care when passing his opponent's lowered lance.

He leaned forward, whispering into Abraxas's ear. "A game made for children. What have we been reduced to, old friend?"

"Blaaaack Kniiiiight!"

A slight squeeze of the knees was all the encouragement Abraxas needed. Horse and rider charged into the list straight away, not giving a second thought to the crowd and the cheers around them.

Reynold smiled under his arnet, the feel of his horse moving under him bringing a smile to his face. The powerful muscles more satisfying than sitting around doing nothing all day. He'd missed the feel of Abraxas's movements; he'd not wait so long before he felt the movement again.

CHAPTER EIGHT

Courtney took her place near the seats set aside for Queen Victoria's court at the list. The third and final joust of the day was about to take place, and from what she'd heard, the previous two had been spectacular. The people coming into her shop couldn't stop talking about the Black Knight and Sir Thomas going against each other with the ease of true knights. Every woman who had come in giggled and talked about her favorite knight in shining armor. There'd been one knight talked about the most in every corner of her shop—she couldn't get away from the suggestive remarks without leaving the building.

The Black Knight had invaded her sanctuary without invitation, and for whatever reason, it made her uncomfortable in a sexual sort of way. Disgust and jealousy raced through her as her mind replayed the events. What did these women know of knights and their way of life? They couldn't begin to understand the time and training that was put into each event. No, they were more interested in getting one between their legs to ride.

"The way he swung that lance around as if it were nothing. I can only imagine his hands on my body with that same touch…commanding…skillful." The woman pulled out one of Courtney's most revealing emerald-green gowns, a sultry smile on her face. "In something like this, that knight with the long hair dressed all in black wouldn't be able to resist me. What do you think, Tina?"

The women gathered around the sexy gown, fingering the low, blood-red satin bodice and tightly cinched black waist. The entire ensemble ran well over $500, and she doubted either of them could afford it. And she certainly wasn't going to rent it out to either of them for the *day. No way; no how.*

"With your boobs falling out from the top, no man could resist you, Sheri." The woman called Tina laughed, winking as she held the outfit up to her friend. "No man on earth would be able to resist you after that boob job you got this year. Big and firm, inviting every male around to taste them."

Looking at her reflection in the full-length mirror, Sheri laughed, watching herself sway from side-to-side. "I've only got one in mind, and he happens to ride a big black horse. If I can get close enough, he'll be riding in my saddle by the end of the day. I've got the perfect fit to..."

Unexpected jealousy had flooded Courtney when she'd overheard the hushed whispers of the women talking about Reynold as they looked through her dresses, fantasizing about what they could do to him. Their description of Reynold's expertise with a lance and his handling of Abraxas made her blood boil. She wanted to rip the garments out of their grasping fingers and tell them to never come back to her shop again as long as she lived. She couldn't. She had no right, and even if she did, it was nothing more than a performance for the outside world. These women meant as much to him as she did...which was nothing.

Shaking the earlier scene from her mind, Courtney crossed her arms over her midsection. Leaning back, she wondered what in the world she was doing. She didn't have to be here today. She didn't have to leave her shop in the very capable hands of young summer help. But she had, and there was no turning back, no trying to sneak away without someone she knew recognizing and stopping her. No, she'd made the decision to watch the last joust, and she'd just have to stay with it. Her palms damp and her body in a cold sweat, Courtney watched and listened as the knights' squires on the other side of the arena pumped up the crowd with their poetic verse. Each squire was responsible for a section of the bleachers, instructing the people there on whom to cheer for and how to cheer.

Talk about men in tights...

There was plenty implied to inflame a woman's imagination under those crotch-length tunics. She was sure each of them enjoyed showing his package without really exposing himself.

The fanfare signaled the ceremony as Queen Victoria and her ladies in waiting entered the viewing area set aside for the royalty of Bristol's Heartsease. Queen Victoria acknowledged the rest of her court, waved to her royal subjects seated across the dirt arena, and then took her seat under the wooden pavilion.

Courtney watched the reenactors take their royal places. Queen Victoria motioned for the audience to be silent. It would only be a matter of moments now before the scripted competition started. She'd finally find out what the female shoppers in her shop had gotten so hot and bothered about.

Although she could just about imagine. Even without the armor, Reynold had the body to stir even the deepest hidden desires. He'd certainly succeeded in stirring her blood without asking. If he had asked, would she have given herself over to him so easily? Probably not. She wanted her knight to be hers and hers alone. She just wasn't into sharing.

"Welcome to the Tournament of Champions. On this final joust of the day, Sir Thomas and The Black Knight will compete in a tournament of skill to determine the champion of my kingdom. Now, let the tournament begin!" Queen Victoria sang out across the arena, a smile covering her face as she chatted with a young lady in waiting before pointing toward the arena gates.

There wasn't a doubt in Courtney's mind they were waiting for Thomas and Reynold to make their appearances.

Umph, the queen probably has the hots for him, too. Seems like everyone but me does, and that's just fine with me. The farther he stays away, the safer I'll be.

Riding a horse dressed in the purple and gold colors representing his homeland of Kent, Sir Thomas cantered into the arena, sitting tall and straight in the saddle. He reined in just in front of the queen for a moment and then pulled his horse around to where his "subjects" waited for him. At the encouragement of the squire, cheers filtered through the boos from his opponent's chosen people.

While a squire dressed in black and yellow shouted encouragement, the next rider sat with ease upon his stomping Andalusian. When the gate opened, the horse thundered into the arena, clumps of dirt flying off its hoofs. Courtney felt as if the gates of hell had just been opened, the way the Andalusian stomped and snorted its way into the arena.

His body covered in armor as black as the midnight sky and his face hidden from the crowd, the Black Knight flew into the arena on a cloud of dust, the black and yellow colors of Heartsease flapping in the wind. His black hair spread across his shoulders and back, waving with each step the horse took. The Black Knight and his mighty black stallion appeared to be one, moving together across the ground.

A shot of electricity ran through her body as horse and rider flew past her, sending shocking warmth to her core. Her heart raced deep inside her chest, sending her a message she hadn't expected. Courtney gasped at the realization of what her heart had known all along. This man, whoever he was, truly had to be the Black Knight of Heartsease...her knight in shining armor.

REYNOLD EYED THOMAS as he sat at the west end of the arena, waiting for the jousting to begin.

What is the outcome of the joust? Ah, Thomas is to win. I must give him the win without consideration for my own conscience.

Reynold tapped Abraxas with his heels. The horse reared and then hit the ground running. This was what Reynold lived for. To feel the power. To feel the excitement of competition. To win fairly and without deception to the good people of Heartsease.

Thomas approached on his gray. Reynold lowered his lance.

Bam.

Reynold's lance hit Thomas square in the chest, catching him off guard and knocking him to the ground.

As quick as it had started, it ended. Reynold reined in his horse at the west end of list, waiting for Thomas to remount and meet him in the center of the list.

Thomas pulled up next to Reynold, shaking his head. "I thought you said you knew what to do? *You* were supposed to lose. I was supposed to win. What part of that didn't you understand?"

Reynold removed his arnet, looking at Thomas. "Thou wouldst have me lose when it is clear I am the better? Thomas, thou must know I would not do such a thing."

"We shall see what happens, Reynold." Thomas urged his horse forward, never giving Reynold a second look.

Thomas and Reynold reined in their horses in front of Queen Victoria, saluting as she stood to declare the winner. Reynold knew he'd out mastered Thomas in every event, yet had this feeling that the tournament would not go his way; the look on Thomas's face and the manner of his words said as much.

"Do not be so sure that you have won, my friend," Thomas said just loud enough for Reynold to hear him. "You're about to be penalized for one reason or another today."

"We shall see if the queen is true of heart then," Reynold responded, pulling back on the reins to calm Abraxas. His horse needed more than this to settle down, and he knew it. Once the list cleared of people, he'd let him work a bit more before the end of the day.

"Good people of Heartsease, it has been brought to my attention that the Black Knight fouled during the taking of the rings. Due to this infraction, I have no choice but to declare Sir Thomas as Champion this day."

The Chief Marshall presented Sir Thomas with the winning ribbons. Reynold watched in dismay as Thomas cantered around the list to the cheers of the crowd. Bowing his head slightly to the queen, Reynold pulled Abraxas around back to the stables.

Out of the corner of his eye, he caught the rich purple-and-cream gown and gleaming black hair of a woman following his movement. Her toasty brown eyes captured him in warmth as he trotted past her and through the gate. Lady Courtney had to be the most beautiful and captivating woman he'd seen in this land.

A lady worthy of a love-joust for an eternity.

COURTNEY SPRANG TO her feet upon hearing Queen Victoria's announcement.

He's been robbed! Okay, he didn't play by the rules, but he still won the damn competition. Even an idiot could clearly see that. There was one infraction. He's being put in his place. Tsk, tsk. Why can they not play fairly? Why must everything be set in stone around here?

Because Courtney, rules are rules.

Reynold had surely won this competition fair and square. She couldn't imagine he'd knowingly cheated in any way. He was a knight born of chivalry, not a man who defaulted on his sworn word.

How can you be sure? You don't even know him, her voice of reason echoed through her head.

You know, though, don't you? He's your Black Knight, the one you were born to love, her heart responded, beating warmth and comfort through her soul.

Whether she did or didn't know, right now, she couldn't divert her gaze from him. Even as he sat straight in the saddle, she could see in the slight hunching of his shoulders that he was a man who'd been deceived and didn't understand why.

He turned his horse and trotted alongside the rail toward her, looking anything but defeated. She stared into the visor, hoping to make a connection. If only she could get a look at his face to see if his eyes would tell her that he was okay.

His head turned ever so slightly in her direction, and she knew then that he'd seen her...recognized her.

Courtney scooted past others sitting on the wooden planks, weaving her way through the sea of knees. Thomas had some explaining to do, and she wanted to be there when he did. There had to be a logical explanation why Reynold had lost the competition, even if it was preplanned.

Damn the rules!

"What took place out there, Thomas?"

Courtney stopped short of the stable doors when she heard Reynold's voice. His words didn't really sound angry but maybe a little threatening. Tentatively peeking around the corner, she watched as each man unsaddled his horse with clipped actions.

"You didn't follow the script, Reynold. There will be times where you don't win. In fact, there will be times when neither of us will win." Thomas slipped the bit from his horse's mouth and then gave the animal a single pat on the shoulder.

"Script? Oh, yes, I hath forgotten that thou playest at being a knight rather than being one. I pity thee." Reynold straddled his saddle over the wall of the stall and then pulled the silks from the back of his horse.

Thomas kicked the wall next to Abraxas, startling the horse. "At least I'm not the one living in a fantasy world pretending to be a real knight. Come off it, Reynold. You're no more a knight than I am, and you know it."

Reynold's shoulders stiffened, his chest puffed out, and he seemed to grow in height.

If she didn't go in now, the two of them would be at each other's throats and thrown out of the faire.

"Hey, guys, what's up?" Courtney slipped from the shadows into the barn, grabbing a couple of apples as she entered.

"Courtney, you saw what happened?" Picking up a stiff-bristled brush, Thomas stepped away from the four-foot wall separating him from Reynold. "I didn't know you were going today; you never said anything."

"Umph, do I have to tell you everything? I am a big girl, you know." Courtney bit into one of the apples before passing the remainder on to Abraxas's waiting mouth. "Besides, you know I try not to miss the last joust of the day."

"He'll want another, Lady Courtney." Reynold's smile lit his eyes with appreciation. In fact, they lit his entire face with a gentleness that never reached the jousting arena.

"Got one," she half-whispered, waving the other apple in the air. "It won't be long, and the faire will close. Do you two have any plans for dinner tonight? Maybe we can settle this dispute over food and drink. What do you think?"

Thomas shook his head, and Reynold continued to feed Abraxas the second apple; both eyed the other with suspicion. Courtney sat on the bale of hay between the two stall doors, playing with a crop resting against them. She'd tan the hide of whichever one went after the other first—but good.

"I know, Thomas, your grandfather is generally waiting on you to come home, but I'd like to have you come, anyway. Reynold, what about you? Family, girlfriend somewhere nearby who might detain you?"

Why in the hell did I ask that? It's none of my business if he's got family or not. As far as a woman, there are plenty, probably drooling just outside the gates waiting for him to step through.

She wanted to know more about Reynold. Asking questions, subtle or not, was the only way of finding out the answers. Even if the questions were a little too personal and obvious.

Reynold leaned over the stall door. "I accept thy offer of a meal. I broke my fast this morning and have a need to eat."

"Good. Thomas, will you join us, after all, tonight?" Courtney extended the invitation but secretly hoped he'd decline. She wanted Reynold all to herself, with no interruptions from Thomas and his offhanded remarks.

"Ahh, no. I think I'll pass and leave the two of you to each other." Thomas swung open the stall door. Latching it behind him, he walked past Reynold with a look of warning on his face. "Enjoy your meal, Reynold. It could be your last."

Yes!

Jumping for joy inside, Courtney nodded to both men. "Well, then. As soon as the park closes, and you've finished down here, come up to my shop. Thomas, I'll see you in the morning." Courtney gave Abraxas a pat on the nose and then turned to leave the barn, her excitement quickly fading to fear.

You are just an idiot! Open your mouth and get yourself into hot water.

What the heck was she going to make for dinner, and why in the world had she offered to make a meal? She couldn't boil water, let alone cook a meal. Last time she'd made anything, Thomas had gotten sicker than a dog. With those expert culinary skills, she'd have a dead Black Knight on her floor by dawn's light.

CHAPTER NINE

Issie slunk deeper into the safety the barn shadows provided her as Courtney swept through the doors into the evening light. Once she passed by in a wave of lavender, Issie stepped into the barn.

That woman reeks of sweetness...ugh.

Issie shimmied until bitterness replaced the sweetness invading her.

Ahhh, that's better.

Leaning against the doorframe, she folded her arms across her chest. "So what did you promise her this time, Thomas? She looked as pleased as an old whore about to make a buck or two after a dry spell."

Both men startled, bringing a hearty chuckle up from her depths.

"What the...?" Thomas turned from rubbing the hide off his horse, his face hard. Reynold stiffened but didn't turn; he was ready for what may come next. By their reactions, neither was pleased with what they'd heard in her accusation.

Always defending the lovely Courtney Parker...

It was becoming a bit much for her stomach to handle much longer.

"Sorry, I didn't mean to sneak up on you that way."

Liar...well, maybe once in a while, when necessary. Deception...always!

As much as she tried to be sincere, she knew the slight smile on her face gave her away. She just couldn't help herself. They were like sitting ducks in a pond. All she had to do was load, aim, and shoot.

"You sure as hell did, Issie. It's what you do best—sneak around." Thomas turned back to his gelding, putting a brush to the horse's wet back. "No one does it as good as you do. I didn't promise her anything, and you know better than to say anything like that about Courtney. Reynold's having dinner with her tonight. We were both invited. I declined."

He didn't miss a stroke of the brush with each word. She had an idea what button to push next, and if she had to, she would. Hell with it, she'd push anyway.

"Oh...dinner. The way to a man's heart, they say." Issie turned to face Reynold and found nothing revealing in his eyes. He'd always been good at hiding when he thought someone was watching. Once he thought he was out of view, his eyes revealed more than he realized they did.

"Isabel." Reynold nodded his head, stealing a side glance at Thomas. For a slight instant, Issie thought she caught darkness in Thomas's expression. Maybe this was going to be easier than she first thought.

"Not reconsidering, are you, Thomas?" Issie stayed in the shadows, waiting for them to make their next move. She was in no hurry. As a matter of fact, she had all night to make them squirm like a couple of teenage boys. "I mean, after all, a stranger having dinner with your...ah...friend. I'm surprised you're not going along to chaperone, if nothing else. To protect Courtney's good name and all."

The tension and hard lines of Thomas's face confirmed what the stones had told her would happen. Her two highest-ranking knights were having issues with each other, and it involved a woman from their past. The situation couldn't have suited her more, making her plan easier to accomplish and much quicker than she imagined.

Good...dissention in the ranks. This could work perfectly to my liking.

Issie stepped completely into the barn, side-stepping a horse apple or two before parking herself on a bale of hay. She hated the scratchiness that poked through her skirt to her legs. The irritating sensation rubbed her the wrong way, just as Courtney Parker did in this lifetime.

Thomas continued to sweep the brush over his horse's flank in clipped movements, causing the gelding to flinch. Issie took note when the gelding's ears pitched backward, and he turned his head to the side to get a look at his owner. Thomas never treated his horse with the harsh brushing he gave it now. The poor animal didn't know what was hitting him, and neither would Thomas, once she got her hands on him.

Thomas took in a deep breath, his body leaning into the animal. "She's a big girl and on her own. I'm tired of—"

"Reynold, I heard you lost today." Issie crossed her ankles in front of her, her gaze glued to the dirt floor. "A first for you, isn't it?"

A stall door opened and slammed shut. A pair of legs covered in black boots up to the knees came into her view. She glanced up and over the muscular thighs covered snugly by black. Issie smiled.

He's come to beg for my forgiveness...another first. Better now than never. Damn, I want this man more than I thought possible. The centuries have been good to him; he hasn't changed in six hundred years.

"Thou hast heard true. I fear I have dishonored thee. For that, I am truly sorry." Reynold got down on one knee, sending a surge of superiority over her. He still knew his place. Too bad Thomas didn't. "Thomas hast explained the rules of the carousel, which I have yet to fully understand. I shall not make the mistake a second time."

A stiff-bristled brush landed in the dirt at Reynold's feet, barely missing his bent knee. "I'm so sick of this bullshit. Get off it, Reynold. She's not your queen. She's got as much royal blood running through those icy veins of hers as either of us."

Reynold sprang to his feet and in one swift swoop, leaped over the walls of the stall. Thomas gave Reynold a shove, barely feeling the gloved fist that landed against his jaw. Both were soon rolling in shavings and manure.

Issie's laughter brought them to a standstill. "Now, boys, shall we just forget about this little argument and get on with more important things? Although I am pleased that my honor is being defended by at least one of you, I'd rather have Thomas in one piece."

Both Reynold and Thomas halted their tussle like two brothers caught by their mother, each scrambling to find his feet and pretending nothing had been going on.

Once on his feet, Thomas brushed the shavings from his pants. "And what is it that you think I can do for you, Issie? For that matter, why would I want to help you?"

Issie chuckled, "Because, Thomas, it's in your nature to help people, and I need yours with one of the bookshelves in my shop. Some idiot decided to stand on one of the lower shelves to reach a bottle on a higher one, and I think it has come loose from the wall. I'm afraid it might topple onto one of the customers tomorrow."

Thomas untied the lead line from the ring inside the stall. "Damn it! As soon as I put Smokey down for the night, I'll be up." Thomas removed the halter from the gray, catching it on the hook just outside the stall door.

"I'm grateful, Thomas." Issie rose from the hay, sweeping her hand across the back of her skirt. "Reynold, you're welcome to lend a hand if you've nothing else to occupy your time. I mean, I know you've been invited to supper, but that doesn't mean you won't find the need for other company, should you become bored."

She knew full well Courtney was in her home away from home making dinner for the two of them, but she wanted to make sure she didn't slight him in any way. If Reynold lived up to his reputation, he'd not turn down a meal made by a woman—especially a woman who reminded him of Catherine Astley. In any case, it was Thomas she was after this night, not Reynold.

Reynold picked up the brush lying in the dirt. "Thy invitation is tempting. As Thomas said, I will be having supper with Lady Courtney this evening."

"Well, then, it's just Thomas and me." Issie slid out of the barn and into the darkening shadows of the evening.

If she played her cards right, she'd have one her knights coming back into her fold before the stars disappeared from the sky.

COURTNEY BREEZED ONTO the small porch of her shop with the lightness of a cloud. He was coming for supper, at her shop. What could be better? The man who could be her knight in shining armor would grace her small but humble table tonight.

At this very moment, life couldn't get much better. Even old sour-puss Issie Cummings couldn't spoil this night for her.

"Stacy, thanks for getting things in order." Courtney lifted the last dress from its hook and brought it into the shop. "I owe you for this."

Stacy, her summer help for the past two years, tapped her chin with a forefinger. "Well, there is a dress I'd love to—"

Without giving a second thought, Courtney hung up the costume she'd carried in from outside. "If it's still here at the end of the season, it's yours."

Courtney laughed at the squeal of delight the sixteen-year-old gave. She liked Stacy. The girl worked hard and had a flare for the period like Courtney had had at her age. It was easy to give her something that brought her such pleasure.

"Thank you! You are the best." Stacy literally danced around the shop, the world her stage. "There's a package from Samuel on the back table for you," she called out as she floated across the porch, still very light on her feet.

"Oh, to be young again." Courtney watched the young lady skip up the hill. She knew which dress she'd wanted and had already planned on putting it aside for her. It wasn't her most expensive creation, and it suited the teenager to a tee.

Closing the shop doors, Courtney pulled the tray from the cash register, went to her back office, and pushed aside the package. Even though she had an idea what it contained, she had more pressing things on her mind, like how to come up with a dinner to satisfy the likes of a knight. Only the thought of the Black Knight's presence in her shop kept her from ripping open the sacred package.

Once the receipts of the day were accounted for, she rummaged through her kitchen shelves to see what she could find to make. Nothing too elaborate. After all, she wasn't Julia Child. No, she thought she was more like Rachael Ray in the cooking department. Quick, easy, hopefully tasty, and whatever was in the fridge at the time.

"Cream of mushroom soup. Instant potatoes." Courtney pulled the items from the shelf and then pulled open the tiny freezer door. "Yes! Hamburger. Milk. It may not be fancy dancy but should be hearty enough."

She popped the ground beef into the microwave to defrost then found her one-and-only can opener. Blowing off the dust, she opened the cream of mushroom soup. Grabbing a large bowl, she combined the soup, some spices, the potatoes, and some milk until the mixture held the consistency of a hearty broth. Once the hamburger thawed, she'd cook it up quick, add it to the bowl, and place the whole thing back in the microwave to thicken and allow the flavors to blend together.

With the night's menial meal cooking away, Courtney slipped out of her faire costume and into a pair of jeans and a lacy tank top. Sitting down at the small wooden table, she picked up the package from the faire's bookstore.

Fingering the twine wrapped around the brown paper, she knew it had to be the out-of-print book about Heartsease. She'd asked Samuel to track down the only copy of this piece known to exist and wasn't sure if he could. It was said to have been written nearly three hundred years ago, and Samuel had told her that if he found it, she'd be coughing up some big dollars in order to obtain it.

Oh God, please let it be the right book.

Sliding the twine off, she ripped open the package. "Heartsease: Life and Times," she whispered, tracing the tarnished gold letters.

It's now or never.

Taking a deep breath, Courtney opened the book to the cover page, careful not to tear the fragile, yellowed paper. She scanned the page until the copyright year came into her vision.

The copyright was 1912. "This 1825 chronicle is as told by the Astley family through the centuries and may not be current as of this publication." Tears mingled with the excitement flowing through her body. This book was the antique of antiques, as far as she was concerned. It was the one written piece believed to tell the true stories of Heartsease. And it was worth almost draining her savings account for.

Opening the book, Courtney leafed through it and stopped at a page housing the sketches of two people. "Reynold," she whispered, tracing the face that had become so familiar. There was no mistake; it was Reynold's eyes staring back at her.

Courtney read the caption to no one but herself. "Sir Reynold Loddington, the Black Knight of Heartsease, and his beloved Lady Astley." Switching her gaze from one page to the other, Courtney's breath caught in her throat, and her heart raced in her chest. There, on the opposite page, was a sketch of a woman who could be her—a woman whom the caption claimed to be the Black Knight's beloved, with the name Reynold called her the first few hours he'd been at the faire.

Catherine.

BECOMING ONE WITH SHADOWS of the night was only one of Issie's specialties. Weaving a web of black magic was her best. She'd found out at an early age, well before the death of her father, how to work the herbs and chants to get what she wanted. Until the death of her father, King David, she'd believed she had Reynold bound to her, only to discover he loved another. Well, she wasn't about to make the same mistake in this century.

Courtney buzzed around her back room like a drone bee in a hive full of honey, mixing this and that until, satisfied, she put a bowl in her microwave. Issie stood at the back window, spying on Courtney so quietly that even a dog wouldn't have known she was there.

As Courtney ran her fingertips over the book cover, Issie watched the power the book possessed awaken. Before long, Courtney Parker would realize she was the reincarnation of Lady Catherine Astley written about on the pages. If Issie's plan didn't work, everything would backfire, and she'd be lost forever. Trying to protect herself and her family name and capture Reynold had to be her priority. If the black arts failed her, she was doomed.

"Damn it!" Issie been told by one of her followers that a certain antique book had arrived—a book her present-day family members in England couldn't even track down with all their wealth and connections. A book holding all the secrets of Heartsease and the Trenowyth family. A book that revealed her wickedness as well as her weaknesses and those of her family who followed her footsteps. A book of betrayal originally penned by one of her knights, a boy she'd kept close to her growing up but never desired.

She'd ignored the warning the stones predicted when she'd ruled the land. She'd become overconfident in her young ability to keep Thomas, Reynold, and Catherine under control. She'd found she had little control over true love. In this century, things were different. She'd listened and found true love was something very few people believed in, Courtney Parker being the exception.

Courtney was in love with a man she believed to be a myth, at least until she opened and started reading the damn thing in her hands. The sooner Issie got the rare book, the less time it would have to work its magic on Courtney and Reynold.

"The reincarnation of Catherine in this century must have very powerful friends to obtain that book."

But how to get the book without her eternal enemy even

remembering it existed?

Issie turned away from the window, her mind drawing a blank on her options. "Now that she has seen the truth, will she believe it? I can only wait and see what she does with that knowledge."

Controlling Thomas became more important now. To her advantage, unlike the fifteenth century, few people in this century believed in the power of magic and the black arts.

Issie turned and made her way through the shadows to her shop.

CHAPTER TEN

Reynold reached out, grabbing Thomas by the sleeve. "Thomas, I beg of thee. I need to understand." His fingers slipped from the cotton fabric when Thomas forcefully pulled his arm away.

Thomas turned, anger flooding his eyes. "*You* need to understand? You seem to have all the answers, Reynold, answers that are as farfetched as the story of Heartsease being real. Why don't you figure it out for yourself. I'm tired of trying to do it for you."

Ever since Isabel had come into the stable, weaving her black web of deceit, they'd been on guard with each other. Reynold recognized the signs of her magic, even if Thomas could not. Thomas no longer held knowledge of what Isabel was very capable of doing to their minds.

For the first time in his life, Reynold felt like he didn't know Thomas. "I ask thee not to 'figure it out,' as thou hast said. I need to find my way back to where things are as they should be."

"And just what is that, Reynold?" Thomas stood with his legs apart, his arms across his chest, looking like a man ready for a fight. "Since you showed up, nothing's the same around here. It's like— Shit. I don't know what you want of me, Reynold."

Sitting down on a wooden bench in front of a small group of shade trees near the shore of Lake Farnham, Reynold considered his words. "Tell me of thy family, Thomas. Mayhap I will understand thee better and this world. There are many things we can teach each other."

Reynold folded his hands across his knees. What more could he do to make Thomas understand him? Things looked hopelessly lost. Thomas believed him to be daft, and maybe he was.

Thomas sighed, joining Reynold. "Remember when you said I'd remember?"

"Aye." Reynold nodded, careful not to discourage Thomas from telling his story.

"Jeez, this is harder than I thought. I must be off my rocker for even wanting to tell you this." Thomas sat forward, knees on his elbows. "I remember a tattered, old leather-bound book hidden in the attic that my grandfather showed me several years ago. I passed it off as fiction, and I'd forgotten about it until you showed up." Sighing, he shook his head. "The first few hundred pages were was written by a Thomas Astley in 1490—an ancestor, I'm told, although records to prove so are nearly untraceable. It tells of him being a knight of service, but I didn't read much more than that. I do recall it's handwritten on parchment for hundreds and hundreds of pages and has been handed down from generation to generation to the family historian."

How can it be possible? The book would be centuries old and worn beyond the ability to read the script clearly.

Reynold nodded, knowing the book Thomas continued to describe.

Sir Thomas Astley had spent many hours recording his family history and his proud climb to knighthood. They'd laughed and cried, as their friendship and lives were recorded for their future sons and daughters. Only now, Reynold wouldn't have any children because of Isabel's wickedness and jealousy.

Mayhap my friend hast found the path to the truth yet hast not the courage to walk down the road before him.

"Thou must read this book, Thomas. Thy grandfather has entrusted thee with the knowledge of its existence. It is a privilege from which thou must not turn. Thou must protect it as long as thou dost live. There are many secrets to be told on those pages for which the royal family would kill."

Thomas rose to his feet, laughing out loud. "Only you would believe in such fiction. Why am I not surprised?"

Reynold stood next to his friend as he always had and always would. They were bound by more than mere friendship. They were blood brothers, and time could not change that.

"In thy heart, thou knowest I speak truly. Thou wilt find thy way to the truth, Thomas." Reynold turned, heading across the meadow toward the dressmaker's shop. He'd had enough talk about the past. "Come, I am in need of a hearty meal and the company of the woman who prepares it."

REYNOLD PARTED WAYS with Thomas and headed for Courtney's dress shop. Thomas's words about the journal sat heavily in the back of his mind. It couldn't possibly be the same book. Everything about them from their childhood until the day before the joust was in there—the death of his parents, Isabel becoming queen, the day Thomas was knighted by King David, the night Reynold proclaimed his love to Catherine. Their lives were as exposed as if they'd been stripped of their clothing. All the good and the not-so-good of the Astley family and those connected to them...including Reynold and Queen Isabel...were recorded in the journal.

Reynold shook his head, pushing the sacred knowledge aside. Stepping up onto the porch, he took a deep breath to calm his nerves. He just had to keep telling his heart the woman he loved was gone from him forever; he'd never hold Catherine again.

In this new land in which he'd found himself, Lady Courtney Parker was the woman who fueled his desire, unlike any woman before her, including Catherine.

It was the thought of a hot meal that fueled his appetite, and it was the aspect of being alone with Lady Courtney that burned deep in his gut. There was something sultry and innocent about the maiden. She moved like a woman experienced in the ways of love, yet he didn't believe it was as deep as she led on. He didn't know much of this new land he was in. He was eager to learn and wondered whether Lady

Courtney would willingly be his teacher.

"Reynold?" Courtney stood in front of him, the door partially opened. "I thought I'd heard footsteps, but when I didn't hear a knock…"

"M'lady." Reynold bowed, keeping his eyes on her tiny bare feet. Her toenails were painted a pale color, a small silver ring adorned one.

She wears the symbol of Heartsease on her toe. The Gods have given me a sign to follow.

Relief flooded him as he stood to meet her sparkling brown eyes. They watched him closely. She wore what appeared to be undergarments. Her legs, bare and shapely, invited his touch. Her arms were lean and muscular, her bosom nearly exposed to him. "I was detained by my own thoughts, m'lady."

"Are they still detaining you, Reynold?" She laughed, opening the door to welcome him inside.

"More than m'lady knows. Thou hast saved me from m'self." Reynold walked through the door into the warm glow of the light and the smell of hot food coming from the back room. "Thou hast saved m'body from starvation, as well."

"Well, then, let's not waste a moment more." She walked into the back room, her hips swinging from one side to the other with natural grace that caught Reynold's breath. Reynold gladly followed her into the soft light that highlighted her figure rather than hiding it.

Reynold stood in the doorway, looking around. There was barely room for two in the sparsely furnished room. Along the wall in front of him stood a small counter with a square black-and-steel box with a glowing light inside and a taller box humming softly next to it. To the left of the entryway stood a small table with two chairs—barely enough room for two people to sit.

Where does the woman sleep? There is no bed to lie upon.

Reynold glanced over his shoulder into the shop, thinking he may have missed some indication of a bed of some kind.

Ding!

Reynold jumped, drawing his sword. He stood staring at the metal box that had once held a light inside it, his sword clanking against the metal. "Good God, lady. What contraption hast thou?"

"It's a microwave. It runs on electricity and heats up food." Courtney chuckled. "You can put your sword away; it won't harm you."

Reynold sheathed his weapon and then reached out to touch the square black box like a child reaching out as he took his first step.

"I hope you don't mind. I just threw something together." Courtney opened the door, pulling a round dish from inside it. "I'm not that great of a cook, so I can't promise this will even be worth our trouble. But something's better than nothing."

She placed the dish in the center of the table. "Come and sit down."

Reynold nodded, pulled out the nearest chair, and sat while Courtney dished up his bowl. "Pray tell, what might this be called?"

As long as it's not from the establishment with the court jester on it.

"A mixture of a few things in my cabinets." She laughed, lifting his hesitation of whether or not to eat it. "I did a little taste test, and it's not bad. It won't kill you; that much, I know."

Reynold lifted a spoonful to his mouth, relishing the wonderful taste of spiced meat and potatoes. Pulling a slice of bread from the bag, he placed a spoonful on it and stuffed over half the piece in his mouth. He'd never had anything like it before.

"Well, at least you like it." Courtney sat across from him, her eyes looking into his. He wasn't sure what she saw, but he liked the way her brown eyes turned the color of dark ale, alive with life.

"Aye, this is much better than the court jester food Thomas brings to me." Noticing her empty bowl, Reynold pushed his bowl away, realizing he'd eaten most of what she'd prepared for their meal. "Thou must eat."

Her laughter sweet like that of a child, she cleared the table of their dishes. "I think you've eaten enough for both of us. And I did sample more than my share before you got here."

Reynold sat back in his chair, watching her move about the small room. Every move she made was fluid, soft, and slick. He imagined she'd move against his body in the same way. The gentle way she slid a book from the corner, as she wiped down the tabletop with long, soft strokes. His body responded to his thoughts of her hands gliding around him rather than the table.

Heartsease: Life and Times. Astley. It cannot be!

Reynold reached over, pulling the book to him. Before he could lift the cover, a hand slammed down on top of it. All thoughts of lust fled in a single moment.

"NO!" COURTNEY STOOD there, her hand planted firmly on the book. She'd totally forgotten she'd left the book in plain sight. She wasn't ready to share it with anyone just yet, especially with a man she thought to be a myth—the same fabled man who energized her dreams of romantic love and riding off into the sunset with her knight on the back of a mighty steed.

"How did you get this book?" Reynold wasn't loosening his hold. His eyes were accusing and filled with suspicion where just moments ago appreciation lay.

Her body trembled. How could she tell the man sitting in front of her there were sketches of them on the pages? Most likely, there were also stories about those people whom they resembled. She'd wanted to read them before anyone else saw the book. She wanted to come to grips with the knowledge on the pages. It was to be her little secret, and now the cat was literally out of the bag.

"Listen, Reynold, I paid a lot of money for this, and I'm not about to give it up so easily." She tugged gently, surprised that it slipped from his hands. He shouldn't have given the book over to her so effortlessly, so why had he?

"I'd been told there was only one copy." Reynold may have physically given it up, but he kept a close eye on it. "Does it belong to Thomas?"

"Thomas? No... What does he have to do with this book?" She couldn't stop shaking. Why in the world would Reynold think Thomas had anything to do with the book? "I don't think he even knows of its existence, let alone cares. Thomas has never been one to look into the fabled history of Heartsease."

"Is not the surname of Astley imprinted on its binding?" Reynold nodded toward the book she held pressed to her heart.

Sighing, she conceded, placing the book back on the table and pushing it to the middle. "Yes. That's not all that's familiar about this book, either."

Swallowing the lump in her throat, Courtney pulled her chair closer to Reynold. She flipped the book open to the pages she'd bookmarked then turned it for Reynold to see. There, in front of both of them, sketched on the pages in black ink, were their faces.

CHAPTER ELEVEN

Reynold stared at the sketches. "Catherine." Her name came as a whisper of air off his lips. He turned the page, scanning the writing. "Catherine Ann Astley died of a high fever brought on by the wet winter months in the year of 1491. I believe my cousin died of a heart broken by the spell of black magic. Should my friend Reynold Loddington return as mysteriously as he left, I am sure he will follow in her footsteps. No two people loved each other more."

Reynold stood and turned away from the book. Catherine, dead! When I am home, Queen Isabel will pay for Catherine's death with her own life.

Why should I wait? Isabel is right here. I must only walk out the door, into her shop, and destroy her as she destroyed Catherine. I shall avenge her death without sealing my own.

"I don't believe in reincarnation and past lives, but the likenesses here are uncanny, don't you think?" Courtney's hand fell lightly on his, feeling like a feather tossed gently in the breeze.

"I must return to my home. By not being there, I show no respect for her death." Reynold walked out into the darkness enveloping the shop, knowing he had no way of returning to possibly save Catherine.

A small hand fell upon his arm, and the smell of lavender filled his senses.

"I'm sorry, Reynold. That was centuries ago, and there's no way to get you back where you believe you belong. Time-travel and reincarnation just don't exist." Her voice small and soft, she laid her head upon his shoulder. "Heartsease doesn't exist, either, except in books like this one. It's a myth like that of King Arthur and Camelot."

"Thou art wrong. Black magic brought me here; it can return me in like." He turned into the warmth of Courtney's arms, knowing in his mind she may be right, even if his heart denied it. Only evil could send him back—the kind of evil that didn't exist in her world. He pulled her closer to him, inhaling her very essence. The vanilla scent of her hair mingled with the lavender of her skin, awakened a wild desire.

Lifting her chin with a forefinger, he wiped away a small tear in the corner of her loving eyes. Her soft, pink lips swelled with a need for him to take them with his own. The tip of her pink tongue quickly snaked out, taunting him. He claimed the invitation her mouth sent.

She tasted of meat and potatoes. He groaned, wanting to devour every morsel of her as he had the dinner she'd prepared for him. He felt her breasts swell into him, begging him to touch them. He was being led into a dance of seduction that he easily took part in.

He pressed her to him, his hardness feverish against the softness of her belly. His mouth continued to explore her lips, licking and sucking with delirious tenderness and urgency. Lifting her, he pressed her back against the wall, her womanhood hard against his groin.

As they moaned softly into each other, Courtney wrapped her legs around his hips. A surge of heat blasting its way through him, he pressed closer into her. As close as their clothing allowed. As close as his dwindling resistance would allow.

Nay, I cannot allow this to happen. I cannot take this lady as if she were some wench seeking a tumble for the night. I have come to care too deeply for her too quickly.

"Good God, woman." His breath coming hard and fast, Reynold held her against the wall, afraid to move another inch. "Thou hast bewitched me," he whispered, kissing her deeply once more before slowly leaving the warmth the circle of her hips promised him. He held her as she slid down the wall, her feet padding lightly on the wooden floor, the light of lust leaving its shadow in her eyes.

PLEASE, PLEASE DON'T let me go.

Courtney slid down the wall, her bare feet landing lightly on the wooden plank floor. Her body quivering with hot chills, the ache in her pelvis throbbed with need. She'd almost had her dream come true with a man who thought he was...

Wait! What the hell am I doing? This guy's probably a fugitive from some mental health institute.

She slipped out of his arms, her heart beating a thousand beats a second. Quite possibly she'd just been in the arms of a man about to, about to...

Grrrrrr! Damn it, why didn't he just stand me up and not come to dinner. Why in the hell did I leave the book out!

Courtney padded softly back into the safety of her back room. On the edge of orgasm, the root of her womanhood silently cried for what could have been unbelievably great. Her head hanging and her thoughts on the man who made her hunger for his touch, she walked over to the opened back door. The night air cooled the fire dancing on her skin. Her gaze on her bare feet, she stifled a scream rising in her throat. The tips of black pointed shoes were planted in the threshold.

"Issie, you scared the hell out of me. Just what are you doing here?" The sexual need she'd felt moments ago disappeared into the black emptiness of Issie's eyes.

Issie stood just inside the back door, her pointed black shoes rocking on their heels. "Long enough to have missed what would have been an interesting floor show."

Thank the gods Reynold had enough sense to stop.

"You didn't answer my question, what are you doing here?"

"I came looking for Thomas." Issie slithered toward the table. "He promised to look at a wall unit that may be loose. When he didn't show up, I thought he might be here." She looked around, trying to see past Courtney as she took a few steps backward.

Hands behind her back, Courtney slowly moved toward the corner of the table, sliding the book along the edge. No way in hell was she about to allow Issie to see her special find. She'd worked too hard and paid too much for it to share it with the likes of Issie Cummings. No, the story of Heartsease was not to be shared with one Isabel Cummings.

"Thomas did not come to assist thee?" Reynold's husky voice broke in between them. He stood at the edge of the table nearest the entryway into the shop, the darkness of his eyes sending a message of warning to Issie.

Taking a step back, Issie cleared her throat. "Ah, no. I thought he might have accompanied you for dinner, after all."

"He hast not, as thou canst plainly see for thyself." If it were at all possible, Reynold seemed to stand taller. His feet planted firmly on the ground, his six-foot-five-inch stance clearly sent a message Issie understood without question. Her eyes widened then returned to the squint she'd first come in with. The woman definitely understood.

"Well, then, I shall leave you to do...whatever it was you were doing." Issie backed farther out of the room, disappearing into the night.

The relief flooding Courtney as Reynold closed the door behind Issie gave way to an alarming tingle making its way up her spine.

Did she see the book? Worse, did she see me pinned against the wall with my legs wrapped around Reynold's waist? Blast! Either way, it wouldn't have been good if she'd gotten what she came for. Looking for Thomas, bull crap.

REYNOLD'S GAZE FOLLOWED Isabel as she blended into the shadows of the night and then he closed and locked the door. Even in this new and strange time he'd found himself in, Isabel possessed the power to spread her evil. As he'd stood in the doorway watching Courtney become a frightened little rabbit, anger had begun to rage through him.

Maybe he shouldn't have made a move toward Issie. Maybe he should've stayed in the shop and let Courtney take care of the situation herself. Maybe he should take that frightened little rabbit in his arms and stroke her softly until she stopped shaking. No, he'd done what his heart told him to do—defend his woman from danger.

"Whew." The word simply a shaky puff of air off her lips, Courtney sank into the nearest chair. "I don't know why, but she gives me the creeps."

Reynold's heart bled, as he watched a sweet woman try to shake off her fear. A woman as beautiful and giving as the Lady Courtney shouldn't have to sit in her own shop afraid of the likes of a queen bent on destroying those she thought were a threat to her.

"Thou shouldst be aware of her evil. Thou shouldst never trust Issie." He stood close to Courtney, aching to make her feel safe without being too overbearing. For the life of him, he couldn't think what to do to chase the panic from her. Isabel had no call to come here tonight, except for one thing and one thing only—him.

"Reynold, what am I going to do? I can't take much more of her and the way she just appears out of nowhere." Her voice reflected the tears Reynold knew were hiding in her eyes. He didn't know why or how, but he knew she was on the verge of breaking. If she did, she'd be easy prey for Isabel.

I would give anything to help this woman, anything at all. I must not allow Issie to take another innocent life because of me. There hast to be... The book!

Reynold pulled up an empty chair in front of Courtney. Taking her hands in his, he gently caressed the tops of them with his thumb. The tension slowly moved from her into him, where he could subdue and then destroy it.

"M'lady, with thy permission." With one hand holding hers and the other on top of the book, he looked into her eyes, waiting for her answer. Nodding slightly and lowering her eyes, she gave him all the permission he needed.

Looking through the book, he searched for a sketch of Isabel. If this were truly a publication of Thomas's book from 1490, then the one penciled drawing showing the four of them at the castle door would surely be there. It would be one step closer to showing Lady Courtney he was who he claimed to be. Isabel was a force to be reckoned with, and he had to keep both Courtney and Thomas safe.

CHAPTER TWELVE

Through the lone backroom window, the night sky gave way to the promise of a new day. Courtney stretched, hoping to work the kink out of her back from being curled up in a ball all night long. Swinging her legs off the mattress, she let her feet land quietly on the cool wood floor. Wrapping a light cotton housecoat around her body, she padded softly across the room. Goosebumps crept along her skin now that she was out from under the warmth of a blanket and the nearness of a warm body...from which she'd done her best to keep her distance. It may be July, but the morning air held a chill from the night's dampness.

She really should have gone home last night instead of sharing the ancient rollaway bed she kept stored in the closet of the shop's backroom, but in her heart, she knew she couldn't let Reynold sleep in the barn again—especially after what had almost happened between them. Between the man himself and the book about Heartsease, she was having a hard time recognizing herself, these days.

Who was she, really? A woman who believed in fairy tales of knights and castles? A woman who took destiny into her own hands, shaping and molding it until it fit just right into her plans?

Plans? What plans? All I do is go through life believing I've no choice in the matter whatsoever, when I do, in fact, have a choice. I longed to be a seamstress, and I am. I've dreamt of the Black Knight of Heartsease, and he's here, or so it seems. I chose to allow a mysterious stranger into my bed, as well as my heart, because he claims to be that knight. How much more in control can I be?

Measuring out the flavored coffee, Courtney stood over the counter shaking her head.

Mama would say I've lost all my brains...either that, or I've been sitting on them too long...allowing Reynold sacred privileges. Yeah, the ones you wanted to save for that 'special' someone. You just didn't learn your lesson the first time around, did ya, Court. But...

But nothing, get the idea and that memory out of your head before it's too late!

The problem is, it's already too late.

She'd never allowed a man the liberties she'd given Reynold last night. His touch on her skin felt as familiar as the morning sun kissing the dew off a morning glory. When she'd wrapped her legs around his hips, he'd fit her to perfection as if he belonged there, as if he belonged to her and no one else, just like the book portrayed.

The book, her prized possession, lay wide open to the page Reynold wanted so desperately for her to see and understand its meaning. The short oratory of the group of friends from different stations in life who grew up playing and taking care of each other was followed by a watercolor of two young men and women who looked all too familiar to Courtney.

When she'd first seen it, her heart had sunk as quickly as it had begun to soar. The man she'd slept with, whom she thought was daft from hitting his head too hard, could very well be the true Black Knight of Heartsease. Reynold's explanation last night of their relationship with each other as well as with Thomas and Issie rang truer to her heart than she ever could have imagined.

It was then her instincts told her to trust in him; to give the man a chance to prove who he was, and she had. Everything, right down to the jealousy in the eyes of a young Issie and the brotherhood of Reynold and Thomas were incredible stories—ones she knew he'd only know if he were truly from Heartsease.

There, I've made another choice. One I can't turn back now.

Breathing deeply, she plugged in the coffeemaker and then quietly sat in a chair next to the table. The book on her table was the only known publication in existence, so there would be no logical reason Reynold would have intimate knowledge of the ancient myth. Hugging the housecoat closer to her, she watched Reynold peacefully sleep in the spot next to her vacant one.

In another world...in another time...they may have meant something to each other. But here, in her time and her world, they were nothing more than two ships passing in the night.

Her gaze moved from Reynold's sleeping body back to the book and the watercolor sketch of them together. How was she going to get her vessel to stop long enough for her to board his ship? How long did she have before he disappeared as magically as he'd appeared? For her, a lifetime wouldn't be long enough.

REYNOLD STIRRED, THE rich aroma of hazelnut coffee coaxing him from sleep. He must be back in his keep; nowhere else would a smell as rich as hazelnut give him such peace. Rolling over, he opened his eyes. Courtney sat in a chair, wrapped in a robe, studying the modern print book about their lives.

Aye, he was home. At least, that's what his heart kept telling him. He'd followed his heart when forced to abide by Queen Isabel's jousting demands centuries ago. That path of deception had led him straight to this new time with people he felt he knew but who insisted on not knowing him.

He'd followed his heart last night, also. He'd only wanted to hold Lady Courtney, to feel her body next to his. It didn't matter whether they did a love dance or not; he just wanted his arms wrapped around her. Could he trust his heart, or would he lose it again in a game of chance?

He'd take the chance. No matter the outcome, Lady Courtney was a woman with more than mere beauty. She stood up against her enemies, even if she didn't fully recognize them. She was a woman who dared to believe in the unbelievable. A woman who, against her better judgment, trusted him when no one else seemed to. She was a woman every man wanted, and if he laid there watching her a moment longer, he'd have to pull her down to him and love her like he should have done last night—fully and completely.

"Thou wilt rub the color from those pages if thou continuest in that manner." Reynold pulled the blanket off and then moved to get up off the bed. It wasn't his regular bed of straw, but it was more comfortable than a few hard bales of hay would have been.

Courtney stood, toppling over the chair. "No, don't get—" she cried out, covering her eyes.

Am I that disgusting that she can't bear to look at me? Was it not her body that kept me warm during the night?

Laughing, Reynold stood, pulling his britches up around his waist. "That brew hath a pleasing aroma. May I have a cup?"

"Ah, yeah." She pivoted twice, as if she wasn't sure what she needed or where she was. Reynold couldn't help but smile at her obvious dismay over a half-naked man in her shop. The rush of pink on her cheeks only made her more alluring and beautiful in his eyes.

She finally collected herself and poured the delicious brew, setting the cup on the table in front of him. "Thou hast read more of our life together?"

Her chest rose, letting out a deep breath. He bet her heart was thumping against her breasts as well. She settled into the chair next to him, sipping from the cup she'd poured for herself. "Yeah, as a matter of fact, I have been."

He took a sip of the coffee, savoring the nutty flavor and wondering whether her lips carried the same taste on them. "Hast thou come to understand, then?"

"No, not completely. I have more questions than answers now." Turning page after page, she rested upon the one and only watercolor of them all. "Is this Thomas and Issie?"

Her fingers glided along the page. The simple act sent his heart into a tailspin landing squarely in his lap.

"'Tis Sir Thomas Astley and Princess Isabel Trenowyth. It was painted a short time before her father's death," he whispered, linking his fingers into hers, the smoothness of her skin soft against his rough and well-worked digits. A slight tremor passed through their fingers, exchanging electricity with one another. Blood rushed hotly through his veins, engorging his body with fiery need.

Slowly, he pulled his hand from hers, taking a deep, stilling breath. Glancing into her eyes, he saw the same need he'd felt moments ago. As in his world, their desire for each other was strong and heated. She moved in closer to him, sending waves of desire through him.

"Reynold." His name floated lightly to his ear. Her lips brushed against his with impassioned softness.

May the saints help me.

Kissing her, he wrapped her in his arms. Her body melted like butter against him, her night wrap exposing a plentiful breast and pebbled nipple. He automatically circled the hard nub with a finger tip, deepening their kiss as he tugged the rigid flesh.

Her sweet, soft moaning encouraged him. Slipping his hand further into her covering, Reynold caressed the firm breast with the ease of a man who knew her body. Tracing butterfly kisses down her neck into the shallow of her throat, he found the path leading to a pleading nipple.

COURTNEY MOANED, WANTING more of his kisses and caresses. His touch, gentle and sensual, gave her the courage to straddle his lap. She moaned deeper feeling the length of his penis against her. Wet desire burned somewhere deep inside her as he stood, supporting her body against his.

With the gentleness of placing a baby down, he laid her back against the mattress, and she felt the weight of his body on hers. "M'lady…" he whispered into her ear as he suckled the lobe, tugging her coverlet from around her body.

His hands roamed down her side and onto her now-bare thighs, exploring every inch of her until he found her moist valley. She leaned against him when his hand slipped under her panties, his body adding more delicious pressure. Her head swirled like a whirlpool. She heard nothing, felt nothing, except their bodies speaking in a language foreign to her—a language she was learning eagerly from a skillful teacher.

"Reynold, please…" she pled, barely hearing the unfamiliar husky voice echo in her ears sounding a touch like hers. She'd never been in this position before. Never had she desired a man the way she desired Reynold.

Her hand glided along his biceps and over the religious-looking scar burned into his flesh. Kissing his neck, she snaked her tongue out quickly, lapping the v between the leather strings of the small pouch just above his pecs. Her fingers grasped the back of his breeches, and she tugged this way and that until they started to give up their position on his backside.

"I, ah, hate to break the party up, but we've got to talk."

Courtney gasped, reaching for her discarded robe. There, in the center of her shop, stood a man she considered a friend and brother.

CHAPTER THIRTEEN

"Coffee?" Pouring a cup for Thomas, she didn't wait for his answer. Her nerves were ignited like an overheated power cord. She bit her lower lip, hoping to calm herself down and take control of the most uncomfortable situation she'd ever been caught in.

Courtney pulled the robe tighter around her, hiding not only her body, but her embarrassment at being caught with a man between her legs. Reynold had already righted his britches and pulled on his white cotton shirt, as if getting caught between the legs of a woman were an everyday occurrence.

I hope he doesn't think this is funny 'cause it's not. It's like having your parents walk in on you while you're on the family sofa necking with the high school star baseball catcher. Three strikes, and you're out!

She giggled inwardly at the thought of running the bases hoping to escape being out at home plate. Luckily for her, she'd never had to worry about such things in high school. She hadn't come into herself until college, and even then, the boys really weren't interested in a girl who enjoyed the past more than the present. She could always be found in the library lost amongst the pages of an old history book, if one looked hard enough for her.

Anyway, the look on Thomas's scrunched-up face was pretty comical, even if the situation was a serious one by her now-defunct old-fashioned standards. The last thing she expected in the morning light was for Thomas to be standing in her shop at the crack of dawn...or pretty darn close to it. It could have been worse. Issie may have been the one to find her legs locked around Reynold's hips. She shivered at that dreadful thought.

"Thou hast risen early this morn." Reynold sat in the chair closest to where Courtney stood at the counter, placing himself between her and Thomas. She knew in her heart he'd be ready to defend her honor at a moment's notice, should it be needed. It was something she felt without any evidence that he would. Not that she needed defending, even if it is the job of a knight in shining armor.

Courtney poured fresh hazelnut coffee into each of their cups. Setting the pot down on the table, she sat in the chair nearest Reynold. The last thing she wanted was for these two to be too close to each other. At least with her sitting between them, she'd be able to run interference.

"I didn't sleep well last night, and there's much that needs to be said." Thomas sat in the chair at the end of the table, putting the pouch he'd been carrying in the middle of the table. His tired eyes looked into Reynold's. "You were right about a lot of things, Reynold. My grandfather confirmed everything you've been trying to tell me. It's all right there in the satchel."

She cleared her throat, crossing her arms in front of her. "Donuts? Chocolate-covered Bismarck's, I hope."

"Not hardly." Thomas pulled what looked like a book from the contents of the weathered pouch. "Something we need to talk about." He flipped the journal open to a marked page. A faded watercolor matching the one in Courtney's new book gleamed in the rays of the morning sun, the painted figures coming to life before her eyes.

Courtney's breath hitched in her throat.

No! It can't be. There's only one copy, and I have it!

Her body trembled throughout from the fear that everything from the night before was a big, fat lie.

A myth was just that…a myth.

Her knight in shining armor no more than a normal, everyday man who'd break her heart on the first chance he had.

So much for dreams coming true. I should have known better than to trust my heart.

Reynold pulled the ancient old journal across the table. "Hast thou come to believe, m'friend?"

Tears slipped down Courtney's cheeks as she pushed her newly arrived copy of Heartsease next to Thomas's leather bound journal. "I thought I had the one and only copy of this book."

Thomas drank from his cup and then placed a hand lightly on her shoulder. "You have the only 'published' copy. I have the original—the one that's been handed down in my family from generation to generation for centuries. If what I read last night is true, there are a lot of things that need to be done before it's all over; before more damage can be done to a lot of innocent people."

"The original? From everything I'd read in my research, the original had been destroyed. There's documented evidence stating so." Courtney sat back in her chair. How could it be that Thomas would have in his possession the perished book that was over hundreds of years old? "You expect me to believe that tattered, yellowed manuscript you have there is an original book about Heartsease? Do you take me for a fool, Thomas?"

"M'lady, thou listenest, yet dost not hear. Thomas speaks the truth." Reynold leaned toward her, forcing Courtney to leap from the chair. His magnificent presence didn't help her right now in trying to understand what in the world was going on. For that matter, why was he taking Thomas's side in this? He was her knight, not Thomas's.

Standing near the back door, she wiped away another tear slipping down her cheek as she stared at Reynold. "You knew about this all along? What did you two do, hatch up a plan of deception to see if I'd believe you or not? Well...*I don't!*"

REYNOLD'S HEART WENT out to her, slamming the door to his chest in its wake. Courtney grabbed her precious book off the table, hugging it to her bosom. As Thomas had said, hers was the only publication in existence; Thomas had the original hand-written family chronicles of life in Heartsease that extended further than the professionally bound book she held.

"I hope you can prove it, Thomas. It's a story sounding more like fantasy than reality." Courtney edged closer to the back door until she could go no farther. Her face and eyes darkened, revealing suspicion Reynold had never seen in her face before. His heart plummeted at the thought of her not trusting him.

Reynold treaded lightly as he took Courtney by the elbow. "M'lady, come and sit with us a while. There is much to be said in so little time." He brought her quietly to the table, pulling out a chair for her. Gently, he took the book from her and placed it on top of the table.

"Thomas, may I?" Reynold extended his hand for the ancient manuscript.

Thomas placed the pages in his hand, nodding his acknowledgement of what Reynold was going to attempt to do. "If it'll help, by all means. I'm too tired to explain it all to her right now."

Reynold placed the old leather bound chronicle next to Courtney's modern-day version. "Look, m'lady, for thyself." He flipped open the cover of the hardcover book to the page where Catherine's name appeared on the family tree. "'As told through the years by the family of Lady Catherine A. Astley.' That is Sir Thomas Astley's cousin. She was betrothed to me by Thomas. If thou wilt only look at the pages of Thomas's family journal, no such name appears—no record of the family names."

Thump, thump!

Reynold bound to his feet, his heart racing a pace that would challenge Abraxas at a full gallop. Someone desperately wanted entrance into the shop, and they weren't about to be polite about it. Automatically reaching for his dagger and finding it not present, he gathered all his inner strength to face the enemy in hand-to-hand combat, if necessary.

"Thomas Astley, I know you're in there." The words screeched through the walls like a knife cutting through bone, gripping and horrific. "Open the damn door, Courtney, before I have the entire faire breaking it down!"

"Issie!" Courtney whispered. Closing both the books, she threw a towel over them before going to answer the pounding on the back door. "What do you want, Issie?"

Reynold took his place next to Thomas, just steps from Courtney, whispering a warning. "We must take care from hence forth." He wasn't sure what awaited them, once the door flew open, just that it wouldn't be a pleasant social call. If Isabel came through the door in a flying rage and harmed Courtney, he'd cut her down without hesitation. She had a temper hotter than a blacksmith's fire and not as easily put out.

Issie pushed her way past Courtney through the doorway, coming face to face with Reynold. "Just as I thought! You *have* been hatching a plan to turn everyone against me. I knew it. I had no idea you played with the black arts, Sir Reynold. It appears you've learned much on your journey through time."

She swung in a circle, pointing at each of them in turn before coming to halt in front of Reynold. A surge of blackness reached out toward him, the amulet stirring under his shirt.

Reynold drew in the white light of protection, shutting out Issie's blackness. Yes, he dabbled in magic—white magic. Nothing as dark as Isabel's soul. "Take care whom thou threatenest, Isabel. Thy black magic is not as powerful in this time as it was in the castle."

"You speak nonsense, Sir Black Knight! I *will* have you, one way or another." She spun toward Courtney, pointing a long finger at her. "You'll not have what rightfully belongs to me!" she hissed, leaving the room on the tornado she'd ridden in on.

"M'LADY?"

Courtney drew in a deep breath, stilling the quake that had tilted her body off its axis. "What the hell was that all about?" She looked from Reynold to Thomas, her words as shaky as her insides. Never before in her life had she seen such malicious intent in a person's eyes.

"Please...sit, and the truth shall be told." Reynold waited as she sat down.

Courtney wasn't sure just what Thomas believed or didn't believe.

So far, her fairy tale story wasn't Cinderella finding her Prince Charming; it was more like *Bride of Chucky*.

Reluctantly, she sat as calmly as possible. "Okay, I'm listening." Leaning forward, she folded her hands in front of her on the table. If prayer would help her, she'd do it without hesitation. There's no defense against what lay in a person's imagination if it is thought believable, if only for a moment. That defense was as flawed as believing in dreams coming true.

It just didn't happen.

Reynold turned to the first of the hundreds of handwritten pages. "It began when Thomas and I were boys, playing in the courtyard of the castle grounds. We were 'bout ten at the time when I drew blood from Thomas's arm in a game of joust." Reynold smiled, as if the memory were a fond and warm one. "Thomas laughed, and then slashed my arm just as quickly in return. It was then we became blood brothers, mixing our souls and lives with one another..."

Courtney watched and listened as Reynold told her about his life growing up in Heartsease. How he'd fallen in love with Catherine without realizing he'd done so...how they played with Isabel in the courtyard with the king's blessing...Isabel's many attempts to own him and his resistance to her unwanted sexual advances...how magic was a way of life for them...how Isabel learned to use the black arts to get what she wanted.

As the stories unfolded with the turning pages, she noticed on more than one occasion Thomas nodded in acceptance of his words. It wasn't until the story led them to the joust and Reynold's disappearance that he actually spoke up.

"Taking your life was not going to happen. You know that, don't you, Reynold?" Thomas barely whispered, his eyes glistening with regret.

Reynold reached over, placing a hand on his friend's arm. "Aye, nor could I defeat thee and have the queen strip thee of thy knighthood. 'Tis thy life, Thomas."

Courtney stood and walked from the table. "Wait a minute. You mean to tell me you actually believe you lived in that time, Thomas?"

Bong! Bong! Bong!

Thomas rose, looking around the room as if he'd just returned from a faraway place. "We have little time before the faire opens for the day. Reynold, I'll meet you at the stables." He turned and left the small shop, the sacred manuscript in hand.

"I don't know if I believe this or not. Reincarnation is for foolish people who believe there's another life waiting for their souls to capture. I'm not one of those people." Courtney turned from the only man who'd captured her imagination and made her feel alive inside. Her common sense would not allow her to even entertain the idea of life after death. Yet her heart beckoned for her to believe in the unknown, to believe in dreams come true and knights in shining armor.

Reynold stood, taking her in his arms. His body pressed close to hers sent a wave of passionate electricity storming through her. Against her better judgment, she wanted him more than anything in the world. She wanted with all her heart to believe his stories. She wanted to be the love he longed for...but she wasn't.

"What day is this day?" Reynold now held her at arm's length, the space between them filling with sparks and a current of electrical energy.

"What does it matter?" she asked, feeling his anxiety. "It's Sunday, August 31; almost the end of the season for the faire."

Terror crossed his face, followed closely by something she couldn't explain. Almost fear but not quite. He kissed her firmly and then whispered onto her lips, "Beware of this day. Beware of Isabel; her magic will be powerful." He kissed her hard and then released her with hesitation and walked slowly across the shop floor and out the door.

A hot shiver followed by a freezing chill soared through her. Pulling open the shop doors, she watched as Reynold ran along the path toward the stables below. How could she not believe in him when her heart, body, and soul told her that her knight in shining armor had come to rescue her?

CHAPTER FOURTEEN

Issie stood peering out from behind one of her bookshelves. There was something going on, and she was going to find out one way or another just what it was. She'd not have that trio win again this time at her final attempt to bring Reynold into her bed.

She'd only been allowed six lives in which to find Reynold and bring him to his knees before her, and he'd escaped her every time until now. This was her last chance to claim what she felt was hers, and she'd make sure he didn't escape her this time around.

Thomas did seem a little more than taken aback this morning when she'd barged in on them at the dress shop. He'd all but slunk behind Reynold as a shield against her wrath. Now he stomped down the hill with purpose, making it more than evident she'd been correct. The satchel hanging from his shoulder bounced in rhythm off his hip with each step. By the looks of it, there was an object of some weight nestled deep inside that leather pouch.

The sacred Astley journal maybe?

With him having shown up at Courtney's establishment so early in the morning, could it be the ancient history of Heartsease she'd so desperately searched for throughout the centuries was in that satchel of his? Could he finally be embracing who he truly is?

Ha ha ha ha. You'll be mine to command before the night falls, Sir Thomas Astley!

Issie had taken a step toward the threshold of her shop of various potions when Reynold quickly walked past. She backed up into the shadows the shop offered her. Like Thomas, he looked to be in a hurry.

His white shirt tucked loosely into his breeches brought to mind a man who'd been caught in the arms of another man's wife. His clothes were disheveled, his hair like a mass of unruly yarn. He looked like he'd just had a tumble in the hay.

She stomped her foot in exasperation as the vision of Reynold and Courtney lying together, entwined in each other's arms, soared through her mind.

Never! Miss Prude wouldn't allow a man in her arms, let alone wrapped snugly between her legs. If she did, it'll be her last time for such pleasure. She'll never feel the pleasure of a man, especially a man like Reynold Loddington. He's too much for her to handle, whereas I know exactly how to make him mine—how to make him bend to my unusual desires and become my bed slave.

"Thomas!" Reynold called out as his fast walk turned into a jog. "I beg of thee, please wait."

Issie stepped onto the platform of her shop, a sense of knowledge seeping into her mind.

Now I know something's going on. Today is the last day I have to get what is rightfully mine. I must find out what those three have been up to all morning. What sort of magic do they think they've conjured up to use against me?

Looking at her watch, Issie stepped back into her potion shop. "An hour before the faire opens. Gives me plenty of time to ponder the circumstances and plot my next move."

In the sanctuary of the backroom, Issie tapped on the front panel of her back door, revealing a secret compartment she'd had specially crafted. Reaching inside, she pulled out her most prized possession—her Grimoire.

DRAWING IN A DEEP BREATH, Courtney stood upon the back stoop of Issie's potion shop. After knocking on the door, she stepped back, waiting for an answer. Every nerve in her body quivered against her skin. She'd never been so damn mad and so disgusted with a person in her entire life.

How dare Isabel Cummings think she can force her way into my shop...my sanctuary...my one little piece of heaven. She'll not run roughshod over me again!

"Go away, I'm busy!" Issie's high screeched voice cut through the wood like an ax. "Your presence is not wanted here."

Nope, not this time, Issie.

"I want to talk to you, Ms. Isabel Cummings!" Courtney rubbed her moist hands over the jean shorts she'd thrown on after Reynold had run out after Thomas. The longer she waited, the more she seemed to fidget. "Damn it, Isabel, open the door," she called out, knocking harder this time.

"I have nothing whatsoever to say to you, Ms. Parker. Go away before someone turns you into a frog, or better yet, drops a house on you."

The threat didn't come without meaning but far from scared Courtney for even a minute. She was too angry to be scared by Issie's idle threats. "Give it up, Issie. Your threats are meaningless, and you had no right—"

The door flew open with the force of a strong gale wind. "Are you sure you want to come inside, Courtney? There may be all kinds of horrible things going on that could turn your world upside down." Issie's hair was wild and crazy, matching the look in her coal-black eyes.

"You're not going to scare me, Issie. As much as you try, you don't and never will." Courtney attempted to step closer to the woman in front of her but found she couldn't move. "You are to never come banging on my shop door before the faire opens again. Do you understand me?"

The crooked smile crossing Issie's face sent yet another warning through Courtney. "I think it's you who needs to understand. After all, you're the one who stands in the way of what I want and what I will have."

Courtney thought for a moment.

Thomas? No, she's never shown any interest in him other than to see how riled she can make him. Who then? Reynold?

Courtney clenched her hands into fists at her side. "If you mean Reynold, I think the man has a mind of his own. He doesn't strike me as being your type—tagalong puppy dog." Her heart tingled with surety she spoke the truth.

Reynold certainly struck her as a man with his own mind and one not easily swayed by any woman. Especially not a woman the likes of Issie Cummings, who demanded everything she wanted. He may want a strong woman, but she knew he needed one who was soft and loving at the same time—totally the opposite of what Issie represented.

"That's where you are mistaken. I will succeed, this time, Courtney. You'll live to see him leave you to warm my bed before a fortnight. I'll bask in the sound of your sobbing for a man who doesn't love or desire you." Issie slammed the door in her face, puffing her loose hair into the air.

"Not on your life, Issie." Finally being able to move, Courtney slammed her hand against the door and left the back stoop with Issie's evil, black laughter following her every step.

ISSIE STIRRED THE CONTENTS in the pot sitting on her back table. "Not on my life? Little miss goody-two-shoes actually thinks she has a backbone. Who would have guessed?"

Dropping in a bit of henbane and lemon oil, Issie thought of Thomas. She would need him to make sure Courtney got what she had in store for her. A good pot of tea would be enough to take her out of the picture for a period of time—long enough for Issie to make Reynold realize he had no choice but to succumb to her.

Satisfied with her potion, Issie punctured an orange with a fork and then dropped it into the pot. She jumped back as the potion splashed onto the counter when the orange plunked down to the bottom of the kettle. Thomas couldn't resist a big, juicy orange.

"With Thomas's help, I'll be able to finally get what's mine." Issie stirred the contents of the pot twice and then left it to settle into itself. "Once the final joust starts, all will be as it should be. Heartsease will finally see me for my true self—a woman who shall not be denied what is rightfully hers. I'll be able to reclaim my throne and my people."

The sound of a pot about to boil over drew her attention to an electric hot plate. "Mmmmm, sweet apples." She inhaled deeply, taking in the scent fully. Reaching into her secret spot, she pulled out a pouch and dropped a pinch or two of dragon teeth and bones into the steaming liquid. "Sleep, Ms. Courtney Parker for all eternity, for what you believe is your destiny is truly mine."

Issie gave the contents a quick stir until the bubbly liquid swirled like a whirlpool. She watched closely, looking for evidence her potion would truly bring a quiet and long sleep to whoever drank it. Satisfied with what she saw, Issie turned the pot off, allowing the tea to ferment.

Issie placed her lizard-skin pouch of wolfsbane around her neck and carefully pulled the orange from the pot. Stepping into the black light, she took in the colors surrounding her. She closed her eyes and watched inwardly as her own body blurred and was sucked into the blackness.

Undetected by others getting ready for the faire, and with the orange in her hand, she walked toward the stables where she knew Thomas waited for her special piece of citrus.

CHAPTER FIFTEEN

"Thomas?" Reynold stood just inside the stable door, peering through the shadows. Thomas's gray gelding stood tethered in his stall, his ears perked, one ear alternating between Reynold and his hindquarters.

Thomas stood, his head and shoulders appearing between the gelding and the stall wall. "Yeah, what do ya want? I'm a little busy right now to talk to you at length. Never seen such shit in his hooves before this."

Reynold looked into the stall as Thomas finished picking out one of the gelding's hooves. "Stone?"

"More than one, I'm afraid. It's as if someone let him out all night long in the corn field." Thomas let go of the leg, tossing the hoof pick into a small black box. "If there are stones in the arena today, more than one horse will come up lame before the end of the day. They'll have to drag and smooth it out before any of us ride into it, or we'll end up with unrideable horses."

Reynold opened the stall door, allowing Thomas to pass. "Aye."

Thomas grabbed his saddle-pad and saddle, straddling both over the wall of his horse's stall. He took a deep breath, letting it escape in a slow whoosh. "I don't know what to believe, Reynold. Part of me says it's all true; while the common sense in me cries that it's insanity. Yet it's all there in black and white—the words of my ancestors plain as day. Shit, even my birth and childhood is recorded in that bullshit book by my parents before their deaths."

Reynold plopped down on a nearby hay bale watching Thomas's agony move across his face. "'Tis much for thee to believe in, Thomas. Thy grandfather would not lie to thee. Look inside thy heart and soul, for the truth is waiting for thee to embrace it."

"That's the whole problem." Thomas placed the bridle over his horse's head, waiting for the gray to take the bit in his mouth. Once the bit slid in, he pulled the bridle over the gelding's ears and drew the reins over its withers. "When I told Granddad about you, his eyes lit up with a brightness and life I've haven't seen in years. With all the fighting between Courtney and Issie, it's hard for me to understand any of this. None of that bickering started until you showed up."

Thomas's look accused Reynold of things he'd never imagined. Reynold had no idea his presence could cause such a turmoil. He certainly hadn't considered Queen Isabel existed in this time period. Not until that night at the Black Swan when she walked in disguised as a lowly shopkeeper of potions.

There had to be some way Reynold could convince Thomas of the truth. Reynold knew it was hard for Thomas to accept that his family had been reincarnated through the centuries, trying to right what had been wronged, yet never fully succeeding. Since Reynold had vanished without a trace, there'd been no record of his existence in their family history. It was as if Reynold skipped over hundreds of years before landing here, in a place that confused and frustrated him. He had to make Thomas realize his destiny was not his to control. It was in the hands of the gods.

"Thomas, I..." Reynold shook his head. The words he wanted to say lingered somewhere in his soul.

After everything the two of them had been through as children playing in the courtyard of King David's castle, there'd been an unspoken bond between them. They'd defended one another more often than any two brothers would have. They trained to be squires together and then were knighted on the same day by the King of Heartsease. They'd even become blood brothers in that game of joust...

That's it!

Reynold pushed up the right sleeve of his shirt, revealing a scar shaped like a haphazard cross on his bicep. "Thomas, would there be a mark such as this on thy right arm?" Reynold walked over to Thomas, the scar illuminated in the defused light of the barn.

Surprise raced across Thomas's face as he looked at Reynold's arm. He pushed up his own sleeve to reveal a scar identical to Reynold's. "How can that be? I've had this marking since I was born. My family always told me it was a birthmark, and I must be destined to do some greater good. I've always just laughed the do-gooder part off to nonsense."

"The mark is there because we are blood brothers. It's a bond not even time can erase, no matter how powerful the magic." Reynold placed his arm against Thomas's.

The scars matched up perfectly.

ISSIE STEPPED INTO the stable only far enough to see her target standing arm-to-arm with Reynold. White energy soared through her, burning her black soul.

Pushing the goodness out of her body, she concentrated hard to hold onto her invisibility.

Where is it? Somewhere, there's bloodroot. Reynold's amulet, of course! How could I be so stupid as to forget the gift my father gave to him as a boy?

Focusing, she pushed the white energy out of her body and reclaimed her concealment before being detected.

Thomas stared at Reynold, the position of his arm matching that of Reynold's. "It's a perfect match." Thomas let his arm fall to his side and then hefted his saddle and pad off the stall wall.

The blood bond!

Issie held the orange she'd prepared closer to her breasts. Carelessness in reaching her goal would do her no good. With two powerful sources of white magic near her, one wrong step would only reveal her to the men, along with her intention to bind Thomas to her.

"Aye, 'tis." Reynold opened the door to the gray's stall and then closed it after Thomas passed through. "'Tis meant to be that way, Thomas. 'Tis the way for both of us to know we were bound in the past. A bond that is said and sealed with blood cannot be broken by any form of magic."

Thomas swung the saddle over the back of his horse, letting it land softly on the pad. "You really believe in that whole magic thing, don't you? I can't bring myself to even acknowledge such a thing exists in the twenty-first century." He felt the underbelly of the horse, pulling the cinch strap under and into the ring. Wrapping the cinch several times through the cinch rings, he pulled the cinch until it was tight, and there was little movement in the saddle.

Issie stepped closer to a stall on the opposite wall, listening and waiting for the right moment to place the orange where Thomas would see it. Not only did she have to remain unseen, but her timing had to be just right. If she waited a moment too long, the horses would pick up her presence.

Luck is on my side, after all. Thomas doesn't believe in magic. That gives me the advantage, and my potion all the more power. This will be easy…like taking candy from a baby.

Issie laughed, thinking of all the ways she could make Thomas her slave. She'd save that vision for another time after she'd taken care of Reynold and his little girlfriend.

Moving closer to the gray's stall, she watched closely to make sure the two men hadn't detected her. She was more worried about Reynold than anything, but he seemed too distracted with Thomas to worry about the unseen. She knew his senses were keen, and the ever-present amulet would warn him of her presence sooner or later. She had to be quick, if her plan were to succeed.

She quietly placed the orange on a bale of hay. Abraxas snorted and stomped his feet, Rearing a few inches off the ground. Issie turned and looked the massive black stallion in the eye, only to feel the whoosh of the horse's hooves before they made contact with the wall of his stall.

"Abraxas!" Reynold stood looking toward where Issie stood. "Nothing is amiss, m'friend, go back to thy hay."

I'll have your hide to warm me at night, you black devil.

Issie stepped away from the stall and out through the barn doors. Abraxas stood in his stall, snorting at her as she left the barn.

REYNOLD STOOD NEXT to his stallion, rubbing his neck softly. "What seest thou, m'friend?" Reynold continued to calm the horse down, not knowing what could have spooked him.

Once Abraxas had settled and was no longer sweating, Reynold left his side.

Something's amiss. He closed the stall door and then walked over to the opened barn door.

Reaching for the small opening in his shirt, Reynold caressed the amulet around his neck. He knew his horse well enough. Abraxas had sensed something that neither Thomas nor he could see.

"Thomas, didst thou notice anyone come near whilst we were talking?" Reynold backed into the barn, not taking his eyes from the path leading to Courtney's dress shop.

"No one. Why?" Thomas slurped, his words muffled and unclear.

Reynold turned to see Thomas take a large bite out of an orange. The juices ran out and down the sides of his mouth.

Swallowing, Thomas saluted Reynold with the citrus fruit. "Thanks for the orange; it's just want I needed." Thomas took another bite, slurping juice as the fruit disappeared into his mouth. He looked like a man who'd just sampled the pleasures of a woman for the first time. His eyes glassed over, and a wave of darkness passed through for a mere second, just long enough for Reynold to notice.

Reynold slapped what was left of the fruit from Thomas's hand before he could eat what was left. "Nay! I did not bring thee that. Where didst thou find it?" The remainder of the juicy fruit fell to the ground in Abraxas's stall. The horse stomped repeatedly on the piece until there was nothing left of it.

"Christ, Reynold. Get hold of yourself." Thomas swallowed the last of what was left in his mouth, wiping the juices with the back of his hand.

Reynold grabbed Thomas by the shirt, ripping it open. "Where's thy amulet?"

"What the hell, Reynold!" Thomas punched him in the chest, his shirt slipping from Reynold's fingers. "Have you gone mad? I don't wear an amulet, never have. It's like I told you; I don't believe in that bull shit magic crap."

Reynold backed away from his friend, knowing whatever spooked Abraxas had brought a bit of black magic in with it. "I fear thou wilt 'fore this day hast ended."

CHAPTER SIXTEEN

Thomas mounted his horse and rode off in the direction of the gates to the kingdom. No matter how much Reynold tried to convince him, he wasn't about to wear the amulet he'd spoken of. He'd told Reynold before he didn't believe in magic, and he wasn't about to start now.

Despite how much he'd read in the family journal about the evil Queen Isabel, he wasn't about to admit it was true. There wasn't enough physical evidence to convince him otherwise of the magic implied on those yellowed and brittle pages. They were stories told through the centuries by his eccentric ancestors, nothing more. Or were they? At this point, he was confused about the entire matter.

Thomas. Sir Thomas Astley.

Thomas pulled his mount to a stop just inside the gates. Turning around, he looked everywhere to see who'd called out his name, but no one stood near enough to have been the caller. He sat still in the saddle a moment longer, waiting for the gates to open.

The whispering came again, a bit more sultry than before.

Thomas, I need you. Come to me, Thomas.

"Damn it!" Dismounting, Thomas tossed the reins across his horse's neck. He walked around the horse, looking at everyone around him. None of them paid him any attention. Even his horse seemed to ignore his circling. There wasn't a person within five feet of him who would have whispered his name.

Now, Thomas, you must come now.

"No!" He yelled, holding his hands over his ears. He leaned against the gray, his body quivering inside. "Stop, please stop."

"Sir Thomas, might thou be all right?"

Thomas turned to find one of the fairies at his side, her effervescent wings reflecting the sun into his eyes. "Aye, go back to the children."

She smiled and then danced off to a wailing child to sprinkle some of her fairy dust onto him.

What keeps you, Thomas? I wait with open arms. I am here for you to take as you please.

"Issie?" Thomas whispered, not believing her voice was housed in his head.

Yes...come to me, Thomas. All you desire is waiting between my legs. Hot and moist, waiting to take you into its warmth.

Thomas mounted his horse and trotted down the hill towards Issie's potion shop. His head filled with her sensual words. His groin burning for Issie's flesh wrapped around his penis, he rode off behind the buildings.

ISSIE WAITED AT HER back door. The sound of hooves clicking on the stones and the rustle of tree branches told her Thomas was arriving. Not wanting him to be seen coming into her shop, she'd instructed him to come up through the trees that lined the outer edges of the faire.

She had less than fifteen minutes to get Thomas to do her bidding and for her to get the shop ready. It wouldn't go unnoticed if the shop wasn't opened in time for the faire. She didn't want any unwelcome visitors until she'd sent Thomas out on her errand.

Tap, tap, tap.

"Issie, please let me in. I beg of you." Thomas's voice filtered through the door, just enough for her to hear his pleas. Smiling, she pulled her bodice down, exposing two round, dark nipples.

Her power was her use of sex, once she'd learned how to use it and the magic together. Men could be so easily controlled when sex came into the picture, and with a little black magic to enhance it, they were always hers to command and get what she wanted from them. She was a pleasure seeker, and the more she could master a man, the more she received pleasure.

Opening the door, she pulled Thomas into her arms. Straddling a leg, she pressed her pelvis against his thigh. "Thomas..." she whispered, kissing his lips. She nibbled on his ear, licking and sucking until she felt him relax with desire.

"Issie." His panting of her name urged her on. He was in her grasp, and she wasn't going to let go.

Taking a breast in his hand, he rubbed the nipple until it hardened with desire. Her neck prickled with goose bumps as his trail of kisses ended at the tip of an exposed breast.

Feeling his rock-hardness against her leg, she allowed a stream of fire to burn its way into her soul. She wanted to feel him inside her, deep inside her, where she'd claim him for eternity.

His arms wrapped around her, his hands yanking her skirts up around her waist as he lifted her onto the counter. She gave in to desire, and she wrapped her legs around him, urging him to take her. She'd never wanted a man as powerfully as she did Thomas at that moment.

Pulling on the buttons of his pants, she reached in to free the instrument she felt power over. It was hard and pulsing against her skin, and her body begged for release.

Her fingers grazing the teapot as Thomas entered her, she grabbed onto the hot plate. She pushed him away from her, her body cold and stiff.

Her breath ragged, she leaned and whispered into his ear. "Thomas, my love, I fear Courtney may be ill. She's in need of some hot tea, please take this to her." The binding potion had been stronger than she'd realized, bouncing itself into her own sexual desires. It had been a while since she'd wanted that intensity of sexual power.

Kissing her neck, his breath hot against her skin, Thomas nodded. "Whatever you ask, I shall do." Righting his clothes, and with teapot in hand, he left Issie in a state she'd not experienced before. The sexual storm had taken her by surprise at first, but once she'd quickly harnessed it, she was back to business as usual.

Watching him as he went between the buildings to Courtney's back door, she smiled, knowing her plan would come to fruition. She'd had Thomas where she wanted him, and she'd soon have Ms. Courtney Parker out of her life and out of the way. All she needed now was for the joust to end as it should have...with Reynold Loddington in her bed, servicing her for all time.

AS THE GATES TO THE faire opened for the day, Courtney placed the last gown out onto the hanging wires that ran across the stoop of the shop. When the faire comes to an end for the season, the story of Heartsease and its Black Knight would be laid to rest forever.

Courtney smiled and waved at some fairies as they pranced their way up toward the gates, fairy dust in hand to greet all the little boys and girls entering their kingdom. The sun was shining, and the temperature hovered somewhere in the seventies; it was a perfect day. Yet, as she turned and walked back into her shop, her heart was heavy. Something didn't feel right today.

She'd given her assistant the day off to attend a family function. Courtney would be alone to man the store, which from the looks of the crowd starting to meander down the path, could be a busy one.

"Courtney, are you here?" Thomas's voice came from the backroom, beckoning her to come inside.

She strolled into the shop, taking one last look at how the gowns were arranged. Satisfied, she pushed through the doorway just as Thomas set a teapot down. "What's this? Tea with no crumpets?"

Thomas looked like a zombie—tired and worn—no doubt from a lack of sleep the night before. "Thomas, are you okay? You look beat."

Thomas pulled out a cup from the dish drain. "You alone today?"

Courtney watched as he moved like the red Machine Man toy she'd had as a child, her parents' early attempt at getting her interested in science. "Yeah, Stacy had a family function to attend. She deserves to spend time with her family during the summer, even if the work here is only on the weekends."

Pouring some of the tea into the lone cup, Thomas pushed the brew over to her. "You look tired, Courtney. Some freshly brewed tea will help you out, especially since Stacy's gone today."

Courtney watched the tea leaves settle near the bottom of the cup. "You're right. A bit of tea may help these nerves of mine." She took a sip, watching Thomas relax a bit as she swallowed. "Where's Reynold?"

Confusion crossed his face in a flash, as if he hadn't understood the question. "Reynold? Oh, *Sir* Reynold. He's getting ready to be defeated today." His stance reflected his belief.

Taking another sip of the sweet-tasting tea, Courtney put the cup down and moved into the shop. "Defeated?"

"Yes, defeated and sent back to where he came from."

"What?" Spinning around, she saw Thomas's shadow round the back corner of her building towards Issie's shop. Something about the tone of the words gave her the heebie-jeebies.

CHAPTER SEVENTEEN

Humming "Whistle While You Work," Courtney rang up the tenth dress sale of the day. She wasn't sure where the money was coming from, but with her register full of checks and credit card receipts, she wasn't about to question it. Usually this late in the season, more often than not, people were looking for a bargain. Even though she hadn't discounted the majority of her merchandise, this had been the best sale day of the faire for her; nothing could dampen her spirits today. If the sky opened up and poured rain on her, she'd still feel satisfied about the day.

Courtney glanced down at her watch.

Three o'clock. Is that all? I've got a little over two hours before Samuel sends someone over to man the store. Only two hours until the last joust of the day takes place.

After looking around the now-empty shop, she slipped into the back to grab a cup of tea from the pot warming on her hot plate. Pouring some of the brew into the cup, she leaned against the counter, savoring the intoxicating aroma.

"Ahhhh." Inhaling the scent further, she took a long sip from the cup. The brew calmed her nerves and soothed her aching bones. She'd have to give Thomas a great big hug and kiss for bringing it over to her.

...defeated and sent back...

She'd been so busy she'd totally forgotten Thomas and his words earlier in the day. He had to be mistaken about Reynold being sent back to his own time, getting it confused with the last joust of the season next week when Bristol closed for the winter. Since the arrival of Reynold and Thomas's family chronicles, their lives had shifted a bit. It didn't surprise her if Thomas was confused. She certainly was.

She'd even accepted the fancy that maybe, just maybe, reincarnation was possible. That it may be likely for souls to find each other again in time. She'd seen people who looked familiar, but she didn't know who they were. Were they people whose path she'd crossed before, in another lifetime? Maybe; maybe not.

Finishing up her tea, she reached to place the cup on the counter. Her mind swirled, and her eyelids were heavy with sleep. Her fingers tightened around the counter edge as a wave of dizziness flowed through her, the cup slipping from her hand and crashing onto the floor.

"Whoa. Slow down, Courtney," she whispered, grabbing the edge of the counter with both hands for support. Her body felt like one of those '70s toys that stretched when kids pulled on it, all mushy and rubbery. Her chest contracted suddenly; her lungs burned in a feeble attempt to get more oxygen into her system.

Oh, God, what's happening? I can't breathe. My chest...hurts so much. Heart attack...I'm having a heart attack! Please help me; someone help me.

She needed to get help from someone. Anyone would do. The first-aid staff could be there in seconds, if she could get outside and into the crowd.

Closing her eyes, she took a few deep painful breaths, her silent plea for help lost in her mind. Feeling a bit more steady on her feet, she let go of her white-knuckle grip of the counter.

"Must be the heat," she whispered, walking back into the front of her shop gingerly. Courtney leaned against the door jam, her stomach tightening with shooting pains.

Sweat beaded on her lower lip. Her eyelids fluttered as she tried to focus in on the room and her surroundings. It felt like she was on a slow-moving carousal at Great America. Everything rotated in slow motion; the outside world reverberated through her head in a mish-mash of sound.

Her vision fuzzy, Courtney squinted to see across the dimly lit room. "Funny, I don't remember closing the doors."

"You didn't, my dear. I did." Issie's voice came from somewhere in the darkened room, but Courtney couldn't focus enough through the shadows to find her. "I hope you don't mind; I took the liberty of closing the doors, since you're feeling ill."

Not Issie, anyone but Issie. She must know I need help. She couldn't be that cruel, could she?

Wiping the sweat from her upper lip, Courtney leaned deeper against the doorjamb. "Why are you here, Issie? You have no right to close my establishment."

Courtney slipped uncontrollably to the floor, her knees hitting the wooden planks hard. "Please, Issie, help me. I don't know what's wrong." Slumping further onto the floor, Courtney felt a strong sense to close her eyes and sleep, to surrender to whatever was taking her over.

"There's no one who can help you, Courtney." Issie stood amongst the shadows of light and dresses. "You see; it's too late. You've drunk enough of the tea to make you sleep for all eternity."

"Reynold!" Courtney barely cried out as she fought to keep from slipping further into the void threatening to take her.

The last thing Courtney heard as the darkness claimed her mind and body was Issie's wicked laughter.

"NO ONE CAN HELP YOU now, Courtney; least of all, Sir Reynold Loddington." Issie pulled Courtney's limp body farther into the back room, leaving her lying on the floor between the counter and table. "I warned you before to stay out of my way. Now you've paid the consequences." She pushed the broken teacup with the tip of her boot. She didn't dare to pick it up, fearful that she'd get some remnants of the tea on her skin.

Stepping out the back door, Issie smiled at the dark clouds

beginning to filter across the sky. *I must prepare to claim Reynold. The time has come to take what should be mine.*

Issie reached the back entrance to her own shop, mumbling to herself. "Now to take care of everyone else who stands in my way." Stepping through the back door, she listened to the conversation going on in her shop. Relief flooded her—customers looking for a poppy oil. Her assistant seemed to have things well in hand, leaving her to her magic.

Issie pulled out the bottles of spices and herbs she needed for the tea from her shelves, throwing random pinches and dashes into the pot.

With Courtney out of the way and Thomas doing what I want, all that's left is Queen Victoria. A little bit of this and a little bit of that in her tea, and I'll be able to get into her thoughts and make suggestions.

With only a few hours left before the day's last joust, she worked quickly, brewing the intoxicating, sweet tea. With the *closed* sign on Courtney's shop door and the message she'd sent to the main office that Courtney had taken ill and was resting comfortably, no one would question why the dress shop was closed. No one would even think to go inside to see how she was doing; that's exactly what Issie wanted and knew would happen.

The sound of shattering glass and a small scream pierced the air. "Issie, do you have a minute?"

Issie turned to find her assistant, hands full of glass and herbs. "For pity sakes, what the hell happened?" She placed the wastebasket just under her assistant's hand, lightly brushing the last bit of contents from them. "You're damn lucky not to be bleeding all over the place."

"'Tis my doing."

Reynold.

Issie's heart raced, more in fear than in glee. Had he found Courtney lying on the floor? "Don't you have a joust to get ready for?" Her heart raced faster, warning her of the amulet around his neck. She must keep her wits about her; Reynold was the only person who knew how to get confessions from a person in a very unpleasant manner.

He circled the shop, picking up bottles as he went along, not really reading the labels. If he wanted to get her riled up, he was succeeding.

"Damn it, Reynold! What do you want?" Issie pulled the latest bottle from his hand, placing it back on the shelf. "There's nothing in this shop that can be of use to you."

Reynold grabbed her arm, a quick breath escaping her. "That's where thou art wrong. Where did Lady Courtney go?"

Issie pulled out of his grasp, shaking off the searing pain from his tightened fingers. "How do I know? I'm not a nursemaid, and you know it. Maybe she's got the flu, or something."

"If her sickness is due to thy magic..." Reynold glared into her eyes, his message all too clear.

He's in love with her!

That very realization burned her heart to the core.

Pity he'll be mourning that love before the sun rises tomorrow.

Issie stomped to the front of her potion shop. "Get out of here, and don't come back until I ask for you," she seethed, pointing toward the stables. "You're not wanted here yet."

"Heed my warning, Isabel." Reynold spun on his heel, spilling a few more bottles onto the floor.

Issie smiled, watching Reynold as he left her establishment and headed back toward the stables. With his untimely appearance, her time was limited. Now that he thought Courtney was ill, she'd have to move quickly to get everything in line before the last joust of the day.

DARKNESS CREPT CONTINUOUSLY through Courtney, the hole becoming deeper and deeper. Coldness, icy and frigid, slithered from her toes and fingers through her limbs. The warm beating of her heart was slowly ceasing.

Struggling in vain to move her body and open her eyes, she reached for a piece of the broken teacup before she slipped into a deathly quiet abyss.

CHAPTER EIGHTEEN

Reynold stepped lively down the path, dodging the crowd on his way to the stable. If Lady Courtney was ill, it was because of Isabel and her blackness. He knew he couldn't break into the shop without causing a stir, but his squire might be able to inquire of her welfare without causing questions.

"Will!" Reynold shouted as he came upon the list railings, his body clammy with fear and anger. "Damn it, Will, where art thee?"

"Aye, m'lord," Will shouted as he came running out of the barn.

Reynold stopped, breathing deeply to calm his quaking nerves. He hadn't wanted to lose his temper with Issie, but he had, and nothing could change that. "I need thee to seek out the Lady Courtney. There are whispers she lies ill."

Will shuffled his feet, clearly uncomfortable with the idea of barging in unannounced on the Lady Courtney. "Is the shop closed? I cannot."

"Aye, but that shall not stop thee. Use the back entrance. Ask of her whereabouts and then return to me with the information." Reynold continued to pace along the stalls, willing his temper to settle down to a soft boil.

Hesitation streaked across Will's face.

"Go! Now!" Reynold seethed, pushing the young squire out the stable doors. He knew Will didn't want to go, but it didn't matter to Reynold whether he wanted to do it or not. All that mattered to him was Lady Courtney's welfare.

"I shall kill the witch if she's harmed m'lady." Reynold paced in circles inside the barn. Every time he passed Abraxas, the horse stretched his neck out to his owner.

Abraxas nudged his nose into Reynold's chest. "Aye, Abraxas. Thou knowest something's amiss." He rubbed the horse between his ears and steadily breathed in and out. "Thou art always a comfort and make me look inside m'self."

I must take heed of Isabel. She must not be allowed to take me under her spell. If I lose control of my will, it shall be all she needs to take advantage. I must not allow that to happen.

Reynold grabbed a brush, waiting for Will to return with news of Lady Courtney. Grooming his horse always calmed him and cleared his head of webs.

The joust would begin soon, and he must ready Abraxas as well as himself before the trumpets sounded. He must not lose to Thomas again, rules or no rules. He must not lose Lady Courtney as he'd lost Catherine so long ago.

Again Isabel hast placed me in a difficult position. If I continue with the joust, m'Lady Courtney could be in grave danger. If I stay and go against Thomas, one of them will be at Isabel's mercy. Drat! I know not what to do.

Reynold bent on one knee, the amulet warming in his hand.

Be merciful and guide m'actions this day.

"Huh, are you ready to be defeated *old friend*?" Laughter edged Thomas's haunting words.

Fool, he still understandeth not the consequences of this day.

"'Tis not I who shall leave defeated, Thomas. I shall not lose again to protect thy name and honor." Reynold stood, placing the pad and saddle upon Abraxas's back, the horse dancing in anticipation. "'Tis my honor which needs saving this day, as well as m'lady's life."

Preparing his own horse, Thomas laughed. "We shall see. You are not wanted here any longer, Reynold. It's time you realized that and left with as much dignity as possible."

"I shall not quarrel with thee this day, Thomas, for thou hast changed. I fear Isabel hast cast a spell upon thy will." Reynold adjusted the bridle and then tossed the reins across his horse's black and powerful neck.

"That, my friend, is where you couldn't be more wrong. Issie is no more evil than you or I. It took me a while to realize it." Thomas opened the stall door, his gray gelding following close behind his shoulder. "It would do you well to realize Issie is a goddess among all women. There is no woman who compares to her."

"Aye, a black goddess. There be nothing good inside the woman. Nothing of beauty, compassion, or goodness."

Thomas laughed as he headed out the door toward the list.

"Remember that, Thomas, or thou shalt perish under her blackness."

Somehow, Isabel had woven her web of deceit upon Thomas's will. Now Reynold must not only save Courtney, but he must look after his blood brother before they all perished at Isabel's hand.

Mounting Abraxas, Reynold spurred the horse forward, nearly trampling Will in the process.

"What hast thou learned?" Reynold looked down upon the shaking young man. Being trampled by an Andalusian, especially one as big as Abraxas, would make even the bravest knight pee in his armor.

Will caught his breath, breathing deeply. "Word is she took ill this afternoon. The doors to her shop are closed and locked, including the back door. I knocked, but no one answered. Lady Courtney may have retired for the day to her home. I left word with Samuel to check the shop."

"She would not leave her shop, Will. Not without a message to someone trustworthy. You did well, Will. Many thanks for thy quick thinking." Reynold looked past the bleachers and trees. Focusing on the dressmaker's shop, he centered his concentration on Courtney. The beating of his heart became one with the thumping of the pulse in his neck. The amulet quivered, sending a message of forewarning.

Darkness had laid its hand upon Courtney's heart. The amulet never lied. Neither had his heart.

THE TRUMPETS SOUNDED the arrival of Queen Victoria's court. Will ran ahead, taking his place nearest the gates to the list. One by one, the squires announced their knights, but none was more flamboyant than Will's tale of the Black Knight.

"My lords and ladies…" Will bowed to the queen and her court and then turned back to the modern-day audience, "and good people of the land of Heartsease. I give thee Queen Victoria's only knight in all of Heartsease who rides a horse blacker than midnight…the one knight who fears no man and loves no woman in the land…the only knight to ever carry the colors of Heartsease's royalty…the one and only…Blaaaaaack Kniiiiight!"

Reynold spurred Abraxas forward into the list. The great black Andalusian thundered around the list before Reynold reined the horse next to Thomas. Reynold pushed aside the roar of the crowd echoing in his mind. Nothing, absolutely nothing, would deter his focus on what needed to be done today.

Until he heard from Samuel regarding the Lady Courtney, he must remain to do battle against Thomas and the other knights of Heartsease. His disappearance would only cause suspicion and send Issie on a rampage of destruction. Reynold had pledged to protect the good people of Heartsease, and he would do so, whether in this time period or in his own.

Each knight, in turn, rode to the section selected to cheer him on. One by one, they selected a token from a young lady in the crowd and then returned to the center of the list. Reynold rode along the rail, looking for Courtney, but knowing in his heart she would not be there. Instead, he found Isabel sitting on a bench next to the Queen Victoria's court. His anger rose, and the amulet against his chest vibrated slightly, sensing the blackness of Isabel's soul.

He reined Abraxas in along the rail where Isabel sat. He needed to see her face, to see the evil that lived within a once-beautiful child before he could destroy her. Isabel stood, smiling as she offered her black lace ribbon as a token for him to be her champion.

What doth she take me for? I am not such a fool as to take what I do not desire. She'll not get what she wants this time. My heart belongs to another.

Reynold lowered his lance just enough for Isabel to reach out with her offering. "Not this day, Issie." He backed Abraxas, the lance going inches beyond Isabel's reach. "Thy black magic shall die by day's end, Issie."

Side-stepping his horse to the right, Reynold lowered his lance to the faire's Queen Victoria. "My loyalty lies with thee and no other, Your Grace," he announced, feeling a small light of hope and joy fill his heart. The cheers from the crowd thundered through the air as Queen Victoria waved a white lace ribbon high in the air for her loyal subjects to see.

Rising, the queen tied her white ribbon around the tip of Reynold's lance just below the cronel. "Sir Knight, thy action is most unusual, and I am indeed pleased with thy loyalty. Henceforth, thou representest my court and kingdom for all time."

Reynold nodded, backed Abraxas, and then turned and trotted into place alongside Thomas in the center of the list.

"If you think for one minute that being in the queen's graces will save you, it won't. I shall defeat you this day, sending you back in shame to where you came from." Thomas spoke only to Reynold, always looking straight ahead. Not once did he turn to look Reynold in the eye.

"Issie hast poisoned thy mind. Thou dost not realize the consequences of that threat." Reynold's heart fluttered as rage and pity flitted into his soul. "We are blood brothers, Thomas. I love thee as if of my blood family. Nothing will change that."

They rode off to their perspective corners of the list, staring at each other with pride and determination. Whatever may come this day, Reynold would always look upon Thomas as his brother.

THE LEATHER REINS HELD lightly between his fingers, Reynold knew full well that Abraxas would wait for his signal before moving out. The horse's training was far superior to that of any of the others in the list.

Reynold bent forward, rubbing between the black's ears. "How much more of this must be endured, Abraxas? Three events and still no word of the Lady Courtney. I wish to seek her out, but I dare not, for Isabel will triumph once again, and all will be surely lost."

The crowd around him cheering and his heart heavy with worry, Reynold spurred his horse forward. Within a few feet of the rings, he raised his lance capturing all five rings. As in the three events before this, he deposited all of the tokens and ribbons at the queen's feet.

Nodding her head, Queen Victoria stood holding all five rings in her hands. "Loyal subjects of Heartsease, The Black Knight hast once again won. Sir Black Knight has won all of the events this day." Acknowledging the crowd's pleasure for a few seconds, she raised her hands to quiet their merrymaking. "However, good people of Heartsease, there is one more event to be completed before..."

A tall, lanky man ran through the list straight toward the queen and her court. He bowed and then stood next to the queen. His actions were animated, and he appeared to be anxious as he spoke with the queen.

"'Tis Samuel, Sir Reynold."

Will's whispered words found their way to Reynold's ears. Reynold's blood ran cold as ice. Every ounce of him wanted to ride forward to hear if there was news of Lady Courtney. If he did, the queen could very easily dismiss him from her court and sentence him to a life that had hastened his father's death—a life of living in poverty and probable disease.

Regaining her stature, the queen stood, looking directly at Reynold. "Sir Black Knight, please present thyself to me."

Reynold quickly spurred Abraxas forward, reining the horse in at a sliding stop. "Your Majesty." He bowed his head, impatiently waiting. The minute that passed seemed as if a lifetime had slowly gone by.

"The Lady Courtney—you must go to her at once!" Her whispered urgency was meant for him alone. "She lies lifeless. The first aid staff has been called to examine her."

Reynold opened his eyes and looked into the worried orbs of the bookkeeper, Samuel. Not more than a second passed before Reynold pulled Samuel up to the back of Abraxas. Pivoting the giant black horse around, Reynold spurred him forward, jumping the list gate as they galloped to the dressmaker's shop.

"Good people of Heartsease, it appears the squires of the kingdom's knights would like to perform a comedy for thee. We shall all sit back and enjoy their merriment before the jousting continues." The queen's words echoed around Reynold as he rode away from the list.

"Tell me what thou knowest," Reynold yelled back to Samuel, people scattering out of the way of the locomotion of thundering hooves.

"She's lying on the floor. Her skin is barely warm, and..."

"And what, man?" Reynold shouted, halting his horse at the stoop of the shop.

Samuel slid from behind him, grasping Reynold's leg hard. "I don't believe she's breathing. The Bristol first aid staff is on their way."

"'Tis not the surgeon I fear she needs." Reynold dismounted, not caring whether Abraxas was tethered. He burst through the bolted door shoulder-first, leaving a shower of splintered wood in his wake.

Weaving through the dresses hanging from ceiling hooks, Reynold found Courtney near the back door. She looked as if she were sleeping, nothing more. A teacup from this morning lay broken and clutched in her fingers. His name was barely scratched into the floor above the cup's jagged edge.

132

CHAPTER NINETEEN

Fear rose in Issie like a squall. Reynold would recognize no medicine in the world would be able to save Courtney Parker. Only magic could bring her back from the depths of the death eating away her life, and he had that damn amulet to bring her back.

She had to do something to get the queen to continue on with the jousting. If not, then her plan to capture Reynold in her web would be all for nothing. She'd flitter away like the sands on the desert if she failed to bring him to his knees before her. Her magic would die with her soul as the witch of Heartsease had told her it would.

She'd have to use her knowledge of this century and her special sweet tea to convince this theatrical queen to continue on as planned.

The people of this time are gullible enough to take any kindness offered them with open arms, never suspecting darkness awaited them in an instant.

With care not to spill the tea, Issie moved in behind Queen Victoria. Daring to lean ever so close, she could feel the fear of death come from the queen's soul.

"My queen, you cannot mean to halt the competition because of a sick dressmaker." Issie stood behind the queen just to her left, pouring the tea mixture into the queen's empty tankard.

Queen Victoria's back went rigid. "Yes, Ms. Cummings, that's exactly what I'm doing, and we'll all sit as the squires entertain. We'll not continue until word of Ms. Parker's welfare arrives. In case you have forgotten, we are all family here. Something I dare say you have not embraced and thus know nothing about."

"Forgive me, for you are correct. I have kept my distance for reasons you may never understand." Issie drew in a deep sigh. "With this heat,

I've made a sweet tea, and it's just cold enough to quench your thirst. Would you care for some? It'll help ease your worried mind."

"Thank you, Issie. I appreciate your thoughtfulness." The queen took the pewter tankard from Issie's hand. "Now, your patience will be appreciated, as well. The entire company is aware of what delaying the jousting event will mean. Reynold has been summoned, and it was his duty to go, much as it is ours to wait for word of the welfare of Ms. Parker."

"As you wish." Issie watched the queen drink from the tankard, licking her lips to capture remnants of the magic liquid.

REYNOLD LEANED OVER Courtney's body, slowly moving his hands over her lifeless form. The bloodroot amulet warmed slightly against his skin. "My sweet lady, what hath Isabel done? Fear not, m'lady, for I shall bring thee back from the depths of blackness into the warmth of light."

"Is she dead?" Samuel's voice came softly from somewhere in the shop, worry edging the words he dared to ask.

Reynold lifted Courtney, gently holding her in his arms. "She's in a deep death sleep."

"What the hell's a death sleep? That sounds like she's...dead." Samuel stood near the cash register, his shadow falling over Courtney's body.

"Black magic hath made its mark on her soul." The hems of dresses hanging from ceiling rods whispered across Courtney's limp body as Reynold passed Samuel. He had no time to waste in explaining to Samuel what had happened—not when there was so little time left to turn back the spell.

"Black magic." Samuel moved in front of Reynold, blocking his way out of the shop. "You've got to put her down and wait for the first aid staff, Reynold. You don't know what you're saying right now. There's no such thing as the practice of magic on the grounds; it's prohibited."

"Open thy eyes, Samuel. Magic, black or white, is very strong in thy world. Thy people have not embraced it and thus refuse to believe it exists." Reynold stood his ground, controlling his urge to push Samuel aside, adjusting the weight of Courtney's body in his arms. His patience ran thin. "Now allow me to pass and undo what hath been done. I'll not lose m'love again to one as evil as Isabel Cummings."

Samuel stepped aside, allowing Reynold to pass through without further objection. "What has Issie to do with this? She's been at the jousting arena all day, Reynold. Even though she's not well liked, you can't go around accusing an innocent woman without cause or proof of treachery."

Reynold gently laid Courtney on the front stoop of her shop. She looked every bit an angel, her skin as rich as fine china and her lashes as thick as a flower in full bloom. The peaceful sleep enveloping her would fool anyone from afar. If not for the amulet, Reynold wouldn't have known something was amiss.

Reaching around to the back of his neck, Reynold untied the leather securing the amulet. Snapping it open, he pulled some of the root from its confinement.

"Samuel, do have a way to make fire? I must burn this bloodroot to turn back the spell which hast been cast upon the Lady Courtney."

Reynold waited for Samuel to strike the sulfur to make the fire. Once the flame ignited, he placed the piece of bloodroot in the orange-blue embers until the smoke from the root took hold. Then he laid the root next to the Lady Courtney, waiting for the spell to turn back and for his lady love to return from the depths of darkness.

THROUGH THE SHADOWS of sleep, the sound of trumpets and merry-making seeped their way into Courtney's senses. The smells of human waste and mildewed hay assaulted her nose.

Horses neighed under the commands of their riders. Hooves pounded on the hardness of the ground. The clash of steel against steel echoed through her mind.

The eerie melody of Issie Cumming's voice floated around her. "Ruin him, Sir Thomas!"

Issie. What's she doing? She's not the queen of this faire. She has no power here.

The vision became clearer. She sat at the jousting arena, waiting for the final joust of the day. Everyone around her dressed in fifteenth century clothing; there wasn't a modern outfit amongst them. Even her clothing was of the finest fabric.

In the middle of the arena, the Black Knight and Sir Thomas sat side-by-side upon their horses, their backs turned to her. "On this day, I refuse to take the Black Knight's life to ease thy pride and bruised heart," Thomas's voice echoed through the arena, bringing a look of warning to Issie's face at the refused order. The snarl made her face unpleasing and unbecoming a queen. She signaled to a man standing just outside the stage, animatedly giving him orders of some kind.

"If the Black Knight loses, he will remove the coat of arms signifying his alliance with Heartsease and be banished from these lands for all time. If he should be the victor, then Sir Thomas will be stripped of knighthood and work the land as his father before him. In addition, the Black Knight shall do the queen's bidding day and night as Queen Isabel so chooses."

Courtney watched as Reynold and Thomas rode around the arena until Reynold stopped just inches from her.

"How can I help but not fail, Catherine," he whispered to the lovely, but plainly dressed, maiden sitting next to Courtney.

Catherine?

Courtney leaned toward the woman next to her but couldn't hear the words the maiden said as she tied a ribbon around Reynold's lance. When the dark-haired woman leaned back in her seat, a tear slipped from the corner of her eye. Something about her was familiar and sad all at once. Was this the Catherine that held Reynold's heart so tightly? Was this the woman she'd been hundreds of years ago? Or was this just a dream her mind had conjured up from long hours of reading about Heartsease?

The blaring of cries pulled Courtney's attention back to the arena. Reynold spurred Abraxas around and charged his life-long friend. The two passed, and Thomas lifted his lance, missing Reynold by inches. Reynold fell sideways, his booted foot caught in the stirrup, his body being dragged to the west end of the arena.

No, it's just as the book and Thomas's journal was written. Everything Reynold has been trying to tell us is true. How could I be such a fool not to believe my heart?

"Reynold!" she cried out, enveloped in warmth as she left the cold blackness behind.

"I'm here m'lady." Reynold's sultry voice lifted her further toward the safety of the light. "Samuel, stay with her. I must confront Issie with this matter."

Courtney felt her body being lifted slightly. The warmth of lips touching hers sent a rush through her body. Her heart radiated with love as she was lowered back to the ground.

CHAPTER TWENTY

A renewed sense of life filled Reynold's heart knowing that he'd arrived in time, and the Lady Courtney had risen from the depths of Issie's magic. His heart pumped hot blood through his veins, fueling his desire to punish Issie for her meddling ways. The woman who owned his heart would live, as, he hoped, he would.

Leaving Abraxas behind, Reynold raced down the hill full-throttle toward the list. He had a score to settle with Isabel before the day ended. First he had to reach Thomas and reason with him before the last joust began.

Reaching the list gates, Reynold pushed open the heavy wooden entry. He owed much to this new and strange Queen of Heartsease—more than he could ever repay. He owed nothing to his former queen and childhood friend, Isabel Trenowyth.

Isabel had gone too far in her jealousy once her father died, leaving her to rule a kingdom without passion for its people. It had to end, and this day would be as good as any other.

Reynold jogged across the list grounds, catching his breath as he approached Queen Victoria. Issie stood only inches from the queen's side, looking like a bird circling its prey. Taking a deep breath to calm the rage beginning to build, he got down on one knee and bowed his head. "My Queen, the Lady Courtney is recovering from a spell. She shall be able to return to her duties in the morrow."

Queen Victoria leaned closer to the railing of the royal podium. "'Tis good news. However, it seems thou hast lost thy mount. How dost thou propose to win the tournament?"

Reynold looked from Issie to the queen, choosing his words carefully. "If it would please Your Majesty, hand combat would truly show the strength and loyalty of thy knights."

"Thou art brilliant! Go and prepare thyself." The queen rose, calling out to her royal subjects. "The Black Knight has returned, and the tournament shall continue! All squires shall return to their knights and do their bidding."

Reynold stood, his eyes never leaving the laughing eyes of Issie. There would be more evil to be dealt with before this day came to an end.

"SO, THE GREAT BLACK Knight has returned to face the music." Thomas stood, hands on hips, taunting Reynold. "Or are you here begging for mercy on your pitiful soul?"

"Be careful, m'friend. The evil of this day hast just begun. Things may not be as thou believest." Reynold sauntered over to his weapons, inspecting each of them for its weight and sturdiness. His squire had done well in keeping them in good fighting condition. But he would not need anything but his sword; no other weapon would serve its purpose.

"Humph! The mighty Black Knight has words of wisdom. Words, I dare say, are as empty as his heart. You allow your mind to follow the fancy of a pretty face, not that of the battlefield." Thomas sidled up to Reynold, near enough for him to feel Thomas's breath upon his ear. "And what is a knight without his horse? It seems to me you are without yours, Reynold."

Reynold rocked back on his heels. "Abraxas will be along soon enough. Thou shalt not tax thy brain on how he fares." Nestling closer to Thomas, Reynold slipped some bloodroot into the side of Thomas's breastplate. "This day shalt not end as Issie hast foreseen. For once, her stones have told her lies."

"You're out of your mind. Issie knows exactly what she's doing and what needs to be done." Thomas pushed Reynold against the nearest stall wall.

The distance proved a welcome sanctuary in which Reynold's anger cooled before it took hold of his common sense.

Thomas glared at him. "You, of all people, should know that. You, with your stories of the past and the present being one. Huh! And to think I almost fell for it."

Reynold righted himself and then took one step closer to Thomas. "Issie is a woman lost in her own power and the power of black magic. She almost succeeded in poisoning Lady Courtney, just as she hast poisoned thy mind."

"The only one poisoning peoples' minds is you, Reynold. You and you alone." Thomas left the stable, his laughter following close behind.

"Thou shalt remember, m'friend, before this day hast ended," Reynold called out, praying the bloodroot would soon turn back Issie's hold on Thomas's mind.

ISSIE COULDN'T HELP but be pleased with herself. Even if it were true Courtney had escaped her deep sleep, she wouldn't have the energy to do anything to stop Issie's plans. From her position behind Queen Victoria, she'd have not only the queen well in hand but also Thomas. Reynold possessed no magic and no way of turning her black spells back. Not even his amulet would be able to stop her at this distance.

Thomas, one of her pawns in the scheme of things, stood in the middle of the list. His squire gathered the weaponry needed to take Reynold out, returning him to the fifteenth century and lying naked in her bed.

Issie shook her head, chasing the image away. There'd be plenty of time for fantasies of what she'd do with Reynold; right now, she had a more pressing issue—destroying his will to resist her.

Reynold walked through the list, head held high, sword at his side. His squire stood at the gates, no other weapons in sight. Reynold entered the battle alone.

The blood running through Issie's body burned her like never before. "Do not allow his show of bravery to sway thee, Your Highness." Issie whispered lightly into Queen Victoria's ear, the words so soft, no one else took notice of them.

Heartsease's Queen Victoria raised her hands, quieting the roaring crowd that had grown since Reynold's return to the jousting arena. "Good people of Heartsease, on this day, two of my most loyal knights shall battle in hand combat. Art thou agreeable, Sir Thomas and Black Knight?"

"Thy pleasure is mine, Your Highness." Thomas bowed, sweeping his arm toward the queen.

"Very well, Sir Thomas." Turning to face Reynold, Queen Victoria waited for his answer. When none came, she stood, addressing him. "Black Knight, what say thee? Art thou agreeable or not?"

"How can I agree when I know not the conditions of battling a blood brother?" Reynold stood tall and strong, looking like a sentinel for a fortress in the night. The trait was one Issie would be sure to dissolve quickly when she became his master and he her love slave.

Leaning forward, Issie touched Queen Victoria's shoulder. "The Black Knight makes light of thy challenge, My Queen. Mayhap the challenge is not worthy of him spilling blood this day."

Queen Victoria thought for a moment, her hand tapping Issie's lightly. "I believe thou art right, Issie. What dost thou propose?"

Issie leaned closer still, whispering into her ear.

"Quite right." Queen Victoria rose, her hands clenched at her side. "People of Heartsease! The Black Knight makes fun of the queen and her court. I renounce him as my champion and demand the following. The Black Knight and Sir Thomas shall fight in combat with whatever weaponry they chose. Should the Black Knight win, or lose to Sir Thomas, he is bound to the mercy of this court." She turned her attention to Thomas, Issie still whispering instructions in her ear. "Sir Thomas, if you fail to rid the Black Knight of his life, you shall return to the plow fields from whence you came."

Issie's heart pounded in her chest. Fingering the small dagger hidden amongst her skirts, her skin grew clammy with anticipation. Reynold wouldn't dare to have Thomas reduced to working the land. There was no way out for him this time. She'd made sure not to make the same mistake twice. Even if it meant ending his life.

If you love me, strike him down now, Thomas!"

Quick as lightning, Thomas swung his sword at Reynold's legs, upending him onto the dirt. His laughter echoed through the cheering of the unsuspecting crowd.

CHAPTER TWENTY-ONE

The scent of burning herbs pushed the darkness further away, freeing Courtney from the black claws of death. From somewhere in the universe, a soft light filtered its way through her lashes. As she opened her eyes, warmth spread, sending the last of the coldness out of her body.

Samuel sat quietly next to her, wringing his hands and sighing deeply. She reached out, touching the sleeve of his tunic.

"Samuel, it's okay." Her words, soft and airy, barely filled the space between them.

Startled, Samuel jumped at the wispy touch. "Courtney, thank the heavens you're awake. Reynold said the herb would bring you about, but I didn't believe him. I still find it hard to believe. The first aid people wanted to call for an ambulance. I had to physically force them out of here."

"Why would I need medical attention? I only fell asleep." Courtney's mind raced, trying to replay what had happened earlier in the day.

In a hushed voice, Samuel looked at her. "We thought you died, Courtney. Reynold brought you back to life."

Died? Why would anyone think I was dead? Nothing weird happened today. Sales were great. Thomas brought me a pot of tea, saying it would soothe me. Then there was Issie in the room, and I was falling... Issie! Thomas!

Her mind replayed the scene she'd lived in the darkness of her soul. Heartsease. Queen Isabel commanding the jousting. Reynold being dragged by his horse. "Where are Reynold and Thomas right now? I must talk to them." She pushed herself into a sitting position, willing the swirl in her head to subside.

Samuel held her arm, giving her the support her body craved. "They're at the jousting arena. Once Reynold lit some kind of herb he had, and there were signs of you waking, he left running toward the arena after whispering into his horse's ear. Abraxas is waiting outside, standing like a sentinel at your doorstep. The damn horse won't let anyone near the place."

"I've got to get down there, before it's too late." Courtney swung her legs over the side of the makeshift cot, her feet landing gently on the floorboards.

Standing in protest, Samuel kept a hold of her arm. "You should wait until Reynold returns. It's too soon for you to be moving about."

"I can't, Samuel." Courtney moved slowly through the dress shop, grasping anything within reach for support. "You don't know what I know. You don't know what I've seen. Someone's going to get hurt badly today."

Standing just inches from her, Samuel stood ready to catch her, should she faint away. "No one's going to get hurt. You know the way of the joust and the rules that govern the faire. Boys will be boys, and they love playing make-believe. They've all been trained well, Courtney. You know that."

"You don't understand." Courtney stopped mere inches from the door of her shop. She had to convince Samuel what she said was true. "Heartsease was a real place in time. Reynold *is* the Black Knight. Issie *is* the true Queen Isabel. It's not a myth, Samuel."

Samuel wrapped his arm around her shoulder, hugging her for a moment. "You're still in a funk of some kind. You've spent much too much time reading and researching that myth. Now, come sit down for a few minutes. I'll get you some of the tea I saw on the back counter. I'll help to soothe and ease your mind." Samuel pulled up a chair for her to sit in and then turned to go to the backroom.

Tea to soothe me! That's what Thomas said when he brought it to me.

"No. No tea; I've had more than my share of it. Bring the book about Heartscase, instead. I'll prove to you what I'm saying is true." Tears pooled in her eyes.

How could Thomas betray our friendship so easily? Did he knowingly drug me? And why was Issie in my dress shop when I went to sleep? Could it be she was behind all this madness?

Courtney wiped away a single tear that dared to escape from the corner of her eye. She'd not show weakness now. She couldn't afford to—not now, not ever.

GETTING UP ON HIS HANDS and knees, Reynold spat out the dirt that had settled in his mouth. If it weren't that Thomas didn't realize what he'd done, Reynold would have struck him down, blood brother or not.

Queen Victoria's laughter did little to sweeten the evil rumble of Issie's squawking. The two sounds blended together as well as whale's oil and water.

"See how the Black Knight has already fallen, My Queen? It was wise for thee to renounce him as thy champion; he would bring shame to thy court. His weakness is evident, even now as he huddles on his haunches like a shameful child to be disciplined," Issie screamed toward the arena. Smiling wickedly at Reynold, she made sure he'd hear her accusing words. Little did she know those very accusations only fueled his desire to rid this world of her evil so they may all live again as they should have.

Will ran to his side, taking hold of an arm as Reynold got to his feet. "I need not thy help. Tell me where Thomas hast gone." Reynold pushed Will gently to the side. The stronger he looked, the better. Any show of weakness, and Issie would only increase her blackness over them all.

"To the stable to get his horse." Sweat beaded on Will's brow, and his eyes were full of apprehension and confusion. "Is this not to be combat on the ground rather than on horseback?"

Reynold patted him on the shoulder. "Aye, Thomas knows not what he's doing. Forgive me, Will, I'll not need you this day. Thou hast served me well."

Reynold dusted himself off. Jogging toward the west end of the list opening, he prayed the herb would soon turn Thomas around.

"Thomas, where art thou?" Reynold yelled several yards from the stable. "Hast thou fled the list entangled in a web of deceit? Or shall I take thy white-livered deed as thy only code of honor?"

Thomas showed himself at the stable entrance, sword and shield in hand. "You are nothing to me, Black Knight!" He charged forward, sword raised to the sky.

Reynold drew his sword in self-defense moments before he'd have been struck on the shoulder. Turning around, he found Thomas stumbling to regain his feet. He stood ready for the attack of Thomas's sword.

Steel clashed steel as they lunged, each giving nothing to the other. The loud clash sent sparks flying. Blades missed by mere inches, and Reynold's heart pumped rapidly. His breathing labored, his arms ached with each thrust from the weight of the sword.

"We are blood brothers!" Reynold called out, falling and rolling out of the way of Thomas's missed assault.

"You are nothing to me but the enemy!" Thomas swung his sword, missing Reynold's arm. "There'll be great honor in defeating you, Black Knight."

Leaping to his feet, Reynold ducked and swept Thomas off his feet. Reynold pressed a knee onto Thomas's chest, the tip of his sword pressing at the base of Thomas's neck. One single thrust, and it would all end. Everything would be lost to Reynold, and Issie would win.

"You hesitate to do the deed. Why?" Thomas's breath came slowly with the weight of Reynold's body on him.

Reynold looked deeper into Thomas's eyes, sensing the beginning of recognition. "Thou art of my blood made by the bond on thy arm." Reynold ripped open the sleeve covering the scar on Thomas's arm. "Nothing is stronger than blood brothers."

Rising, Reynold freed Thomas. He turned his back to Thomas, hoping he'd realize their fate lay in his next move. He could feel Thomas's presence behind him. Confusion as to what he should do next seeped from his mind.

Reynold remained standing, his back to a man he'd give his own life for; a man he loved as if he were his own brother from their mother's womb, a man he trusted even now.

"Kill him, Sir Thomas!" Issie's shrilled command broke through the silence of the watching crowd. "Kill him now!"

Thomas moved in closer to Reynold. He could feel Thomas's breath upon the back of his neck. "If thou art up to the task, make it swift, my brother."

"*No!*" Courtney's cry echoed into the arena, followed by the sound of thundering hooves.

THE MIGHTY ANDALUSIAN leaped easily over the gates, never missing a step. Halting in a sliding stop at Reynold's shoulder, Courtney slid to the ground from the horse's back.

"Thomas, think about what you're doing." Courtney's voice sounded soft and soothing to her own ears. Now if only she could convince Thomas to relinquish his hold of Reynold, they all might get through this without a scratch. "Issie has bewitched you. I don't know how or why, but she has. Just like when she sent you to give me the tea. Do you remember that Thomas? The tea was poisoned somehow. Reynold saved me, just as he's trying to save you now."

Reynold reached out for her arm, his eyes pleading with her. "Thou must leave the list, Lady Courtney. This is no place for thee."

Thomas grabbed Reynold around the neck, securing him in place. "I remember well, Reynold. I, alone, must undo the damage done this day. Forgive me, brother," he whispered.

Reynold stiffened. "You cannot do this alone," he stated, even as the hold tightened around his neck.

"Thomas, please. I beg of you." Courtney stepped closer, tears trailing down her cheeks. She had to put a stop to this madness. "People of Heartsease, dost thou wish to witness one knight slay another without honor?"

The cheering crowd did nothing to raise her hopes. They were blind to what was really happening before their eyes. They all believed it was part of the performance today, nearly the last day of the season.

Issie jumped from her position at the queen's side into the arena, her skirts billowing behind her. "Kill him, Thomas, and you can do what you will with the Lady Courtney. I give her to you." Her breath landed on Courtney's ear. "She'll be a prize worth taking, don't you agree?"

Courtney shook her head, fear running rampant through her. "No, Thomas. Please don't do this. You don't have to do this."

"Do it, Thomas, or I shall run my knife through her," Issie hissed, pressing the tip of a dagger into Courtney's ribcage.

"As you wish." Thomas bowed his head, and with the swiftness of a cat, he hit Reynold in the head with the back of his sword. Reynold fell to the ground, limp.

"Oh God, Thomas!" Courtney's cry flew through the arena. The crowd cheered, urging the scene below them to be played out fully.

"I give you the Black Knight to do with as you please," Thomas said, kicking aside one of Reynold's legs. "Now give me the Lady Courtney."

"Do you think me the fool, Thomas? Give you the one thing in this world that gives Reynold love?" Issie pressed the knife closer into Courtney's ribs.

"No. No, please. I'll do anything you say," Courtney pleaded, not knowing whether Thomas was with them. Something about the momentary sparkle in his eye gave her hope.

Thomas grabbed Courtney's arm, yanking her away from Issie. "She's mine, Issie. My friend, my confidant, and my blood brother's love."

As if on signal, Reynold rose up and grabbed Issie's hand. Pulling her down, he brought her to the ground on top of him.

A moan of surprise escaped her. "Why, Reynold?" she asked as her mortal body turned to ashes and drifted away with the wind.

Cheers roared through the arena. Queen Victoria and her court sat mystified.

Courtney helped Reynold to his feet, steadying him as he took a step. Wrapping an arm around her shoulder, he held her tight. Courtney nestled in closer, the warmth of his body igniting hers.

Looking down into her eyes, he smiled sweetly through the pain of injury. "Tell me, fair lady, do we know each other?" Reynold stopped, lifting her chin to peer deeper into her eyes. "I feel as though I should know you well."

"I believe, sir, our paths may have crossed at another faire long, long ago in another time and another place." His heart beat in rhythm with hers, as if they were one.

"I believe you are right, Lady Courtney." His head tilted slightly. Their lips met with sweet passion.

With Abraxas following behind, she knew right then and there...she'd truly met her Black Knight of Heartsease.

THE END

MEDIEVAL GLOSSARY OF PHRASES, TERMS AND EXPRESSIONS

Medieval Wordbook, Madeleine Pelner Cosman
A Knight and His Horse, Second Edition, Ewart Oakeshott

ARCON = front of war-saddle that curves upward; wooden framework of saddle tree

arnet = fifteenth-century helmet

aroint = away

art = are

bannock = a flaky, gritty, unleavened barley, pease or wheat bread often embellished with glazed fruit and currants

bard = horse's armor; protective meal plates for a horse's neck, breast, or flank

caparison = horse's ornamental and ceremonial blanket or costume

cronel = special head shaped like a crown with no sharpened edges fitted to lances; used to joust *à plaisance*

ergotism = a disease caused by fungal changes in rye grain seed

Grimoire = book of spells, potions

grammarcy = thank you

Joust à plaisance = jousting for pleasure; competition

list = jousting arena

love-jousting = sexual intercourse

mail = flexible armor, consisting rings linked together; small exterior plates

nay = no

ne'r = never

salmagundi = a mixed, aromatic stew, combining several meats, vegetables and spices

thou = you

thy = your/the

tilt = long barrier extending the full length of the lists separating competitors, affording extra protection to each competitor

wherefore = why

ABOUT THE AUTHOR

MAXINE DOUGLAS FIRST began writing in the early 1970s while in high school. She took every creative writing course that was offered (grammar was not her best course) at the time and focused her energy for many, many years after that time on poetry. When a dear friend's sister revealed she was going to become a published romance author, that was all Maxine needed to get the ball rolling. She finished her first manuscript in a month's time.

Maxine currently resides in Oklahoma and is a member of the Oklahoma Writer's Federation, Inc.

One of the many things Maxine has learned over the years of her life is that you can never stop dreaming and reaching for the stars, because sooner or later, you'll touch one, and it'll bring you more happiness than you can ever imagine. She feels lucky and blessed, over the past several years, to have been able to reach out and touch the stars—and she's still reaching.

Maxine loves hearing from her readers. All you have to do is catch her on Facebook, X (fka Twitter), and/or Instagram. Come on over and say "Hello."